Her Own Place

Also by Dori Sanders

CLOVER

DORI SANDERS

Her Own Place

a novel

Algonquin Books of Chapel Hill

1993

Published by

Algonquin Books of Chapel Hill

Post Office Box 2225

Chapel Hill, North Carolina 27515-2225

a division of

Workman Publishing Company, Inc.

708 Broadway

New York, New York 10003

This is a work of fiction. All names, characters, places, and incidents are either products of the author's imagination or are used ficticiously. No reference to any real person is intended or should be inferred.

Library of Congress Cataloging-in-Publication Data

Sanders, Dori, 1934–

  Her Own Place : a novel / by Dori Sanders.

    p. cm.

  ISBN 1-56512-027-2

  I. Title.

PS3569.A4877L3   1993

813'.54—dc20   92-34208 CIP

To my friends and neighbors in York County, South Carolina,
and all over the country, who have encouraged me.

Her Own Place

Part : I

: 1 :

The house was new, but an old person lived in it. There were all the visible signs. A young person would have followed the carefully balanced landscape plan of the builder, but these flowers and shrubs were carted in from the old place, planted like browning snapshots in a poorly arranged old photo album, a little ragged around the edges and straggly, like orphan plants with their support systems removed. The plants were very much like the owner of the house, a woman named Mae Lee Barnes. Her children, who had grown up surrounding her like plants in a carefully tended perennial bed, had removed themselves and left visible the now uneven edges of her life.

Mae Lee fingered the virgin brass doorknob on the heavy front door with set-in panels, thinking how grand it would have been for her children if they had been able to grow up in this new house. She smiled at the thought of her pretty daughters, dressed in their Sunday best, spending long summer afternoons on the front porch with their Sunday visitors.

But at least now, through their generosity in helping her build it, this new house would be there for them and their children.

She walked inside, leaned against the closed door, and gazed at the clutter. She felt crowded by the abundant display of things, a collection which seemed to belong to someone who had lived for a very long time. She had moved an old past into a new house. It made her feel older than her years, old in mind.

She felt a twinge of guilt. Spring was almost over and she had not cleaned a single room. She couldn't help thinking, What would my mama say? For years she'd carried out the same yearly rituals as her mother and generations of others before her. Spring cleaning, with all the winter garments and blankets hung outside for airing, then heavily seeded with mothballs, and in spite of it all, always sprinkled with moth-eaten holes by winter. These seasonal habits were performed with the exactness of migrating birds renewing their contract with the returning spring.

She looked at several Cardui calendars, each offering a different year. Old reading mixed with new. Black Draught, a favorite laxative for generations. Syrup of Black Draught for children "when child's play is not fun." Bold advertising splashes of Cardui formulas for women on "certain days" competed with ads for ointments to rub on for gardening pains.

She briefly studied the wall where the pictures of Jesus with a halo around his head, Martin Luther King, Jr., and John F. Kennedy had hung, spaces now empty because Amberlee, one of her visiting "decorating" daughters, had taken them down. She had never been able to understand why her daughter

4

left the old-timey Cardui calendars hanging. Maybe she had known her mama could not do without her planting charts.

Mae Lee knew it bothered her daughters that she held on to so many things. Sometimes it bothered her as well. Sometimes she even chafed at being locked into playing out the role of her mama's life. Why do I feel I'm duty bound to keep holding on to so many things my mama left behind? she thought.

An image popped into her mind: a small child standing next to her mama as she lovingly cleaned the cherished things and reminded her little daughter, "Now you remember, child, this bowl belonged to your grandmother. They didn't have many pretty things like this and it was passed down to me for safekeeping."

Even more vivid was the memory of a long-unused, scuffed suitcase, not on display but tucked away in a corner of the closet in her bedroom, with the nightgowns still in it that her mama had taken to the hospital in her final days. The gowns had been in that suitcase over twenty years. She could not say why she was unable to dispose of them. In truth, when she had moved to the new house, the largest thing in the van had been the presence of her mama.

Mae Lee listened to music as she moved about her new house, opening windows. She had a new radio—two of them, counting the bedside clock radio her grandchildren gave her —yet she played the old wood-encased Philco. She kept it turned to a station that played the old hit tunes she liked so well, songs that edged out the new things in her life, even the new house. Her thoughts so often remained in the past. She felt dated, stuck in an old world.

A breeze moved through the house. At least the rooms would get aired out. Her mama would have approved of that.

She glanced at the clock. It was almost four in the afternoon. There was something she didn't want to miss on the "Oprah Winfrey Show." The picture on the television flashed on, then off. The cable was out again. Now everything else would be out too. For a few minutes she studied the snow on the TV set. Blurred grayish white spots intermingled with black, shimmering across the screen.

It seemed like every time there was something she especially wanted to see, the cable was out. She reached for the phone directory to call and complain, then changed her mind. She turned on her reliable old radio, leaned back in her favorite recliner, and let her thoughts just go on and flow into the past.

: 2 :

There was a time when she didn't have even a reliable radio. She remembered one day in particular. It was in 1941, December seventh, to be exact, shortly after her sixteenth birthday. When the sound of ringing iron bells filled the quiet Sunday air, her mama had struggled to get their old battery-powered radio to play, but the batteries were dead. Even though she'd tried wedging a copper penny in the end, nothing helped. On that day it seemed every bell in the rural countryside was ringing. Usually that meant something dreadful had happened.

Mae Lee had stood with her mama and daddy on the front porch of their house. They had stood there, their eyes searching the winding dirt road that led to the house for some clue to the disturbance. Her daddy knew only that whatever news it was, he should try to pass it on. He had started down the steps to ring their own heavy iron bell mounted on a sturdy cedar post next to the meat smokehouse when they spotted

Bennie Sims's old T-Model Ford car rounding the curve. Bennie braked to a screeching halt, but didn't turn the engine off. "We're at war, Sam," he shouted, "we're at war with the Japanese," and was off on his way to another farmhouse.

Sam Hudson bought new batteries for the radio, and every night after supper the radio was placed on the table. They would sit and listen, hanging on to every word about the war.

After the Pearl Harbor bombing, the United States also declared war on Germany. Fear gripped the nation. In the rural farming community "war" was on the tip of everyone's tongue. The menfolk, young and old, were pulled from homes and shipped off to camps, then moved overseas. Many of the women went to work in a munitions plant in nearby North Carolina.

Mae Lee and her girlfriends were finding it hard to concentrate during their senior year in high school. It seemed that all the boys in the eleventh grade were eighteen or over, and were either being drafted or enlisting. Jeff Barnes, the young man Mae Lee was hoping would start courting her, was going on nineteen. She'd had her eyes set on him long before the war started.

At a picnic the summer before, Jeff Barnes had held her hand for a long time, looking at her with his light caramel eyes, not even letting go when Ludie Gray, the most popular girl in Tally County, South Carolina, invited him to a box supper her mama was having. He still held on to her hand, and asked, "May I bring Mae Lee?" and she was on cloud nine for weeks.

When Jeff Barnes sent a handwritten note to her by her friend Ellabelle Jenkins, a note that read, "Will you please be my sweetheart?" Mae Lee knew she was in love. The weather outside was certainly not as warm as her inner feelings. The sunlight was bleak, like the war news. Mae Lee and Ella-belle had stayed after school working on a class project and it was nearly dark before they headed home. They buttoned their well-worn everyday winter coats and pulled their wool knit caps down to their eyebrows. It was cold, and the dark cloudy sky caused the winter darkness to move in even earlier. The frosty ground crunched beneath their feet as they hurried along. They'd have just enough daylight to take the shortcut over the train trestle above a rushing stream.

"I know how you can help win the war," Ellabelle blurted out. "Marry the one you dearly love. It will make him fight harder to come back to you." She dropped her voice to a whis-per, and made Mae Lee promise not to tell a soul that she was going to marry Leroy Ellis, one of their enlisted class-mates. Mae Lee felt warm tears stream down her cold face. "What about school? What about me? I won't have any friends left," she said. She felt better when Ellabelle assured her she wouldn't be moving away. She would still live with her folks on the farm next to Mae Lee, in one of Mr. Jay Granger's houses.

"I don't suppose Jeff Barnes will ever ask me to marry him," Mae Lee said sadly.

"I bet he will and soon. Remember your love note?"

Mae Lee brightened and later at home read and reread the note. She listened to the radio and solo-danced until her daddy came home. She held on to a broom, pretending it was a zoot-suited Jeff Barnes, and then twirled away to the beat of "In the Mood" and "One O'clock Jump."

Ellabelle had been right. Jeff Barnes did tell Mae Lee that he was going to ask her daddy for her hand in marriage if she said yes. And, when he did propose, as she later learned when comparing notes with her girlfriends, he used exactly the same words that he and the other boys had learned from a class play: "It has long been my intention to ask you a very important question . . ."

Mae Lee knew that the big problem in getting her parents' consent to marry would be her daddy. It would be easy with her mama. All she had to do was approach her at her most tired moment, which was at 11:00 p.m. after she came home from working a double shift at the munitions plant.

On a Wednesday two weeks later, Mae Lee's mama worked late, and Mae Lee was waiting. A hot fire blazed in the potbellied stove just off her tiny bedroom. The little house was warm and cozy, yet Mae Lee shivered beneath the heavy patchwork quilts. She heard the front door open and close. The usual scene played in her mind. Her daddy would head for bed. In the dim flickering light of the smoked globes of the kerosene lamps, her mama would take the plate that had been fixed for her from the wood-stove warmers and listen to the radio while she ate her supper. Sometimes she would doze off, her head, cradled on her arms, drooped across the big, black King James Bible.

Mae Lee never had to look to know it was turned to Proverbs

31:10. There was no picture for these pages. The story of the woman to be praised was a picture in itself. She knew how her mama had tried to fashion her life after that woman. "She considereth a field, and buyeth it: with the fruit of her hands she planteth a vineyard . . . her candle goeth not out by night. . . . She looketh well to the ways of her household, and eateth not the bread of idleness. Her children arise up, and call her blessed; her husband also, and praiseth her." Her mama had been the one who bought the farm they lived on. But her mama never spoke about it. She hadn't even told her own daughter about it. Her daddy had told her. He was proud of his wife's strength and courage.

That Wednesday night the routine held. Mae Lee eased into a chair next to her tired mama, and gently shook her. "Wake up, Mama," she said softly. "It's time to go to bed." Her mama stirred and turned off the radio. By then the station had gone off the air and there was only static.

"I milked Starlight really good this week, Mama. Stripped all the milk out of her teats. Her milk won't dry up like Miss Anna's cow. Starlight will stay fresh for a long time."

Her mama sleepily smiled up at her. "You are a good girl, Mae Lee."

Vergie Hudson stood up and closed the dampers on the wood stove. Mae Lee stood so close behind, her mama bumped into her when she turned.

"Mama, I want to get married," Mae Lee blurted out. When her mama didn't answer, she asked, "Did you hear me, Mama?"

"Yes, honey. It's good to get married." She grabbed her back. "Oh, my poor aching back."

"Mama, I mean I want to marry now, before every boy in Rising Ridge goes off to fight. Please, Mama, please let me."

"You have anyone in particular in mind, child?"

"Yes, ma'am. Jeff Barnes."

"Well, he seems like a right decent young man." Her mama picked up the kerosene lamp. "If it's all right with your daddy, it's all right with me, honey." Mae Lee smiled an inner smile and started planning as she followed her mother's tired form. Before she opened her bedroom door, Vergie turned to face Mae Lee. "You best let your daddy know you've started keeping company with Jeff Barnes before you bring up marriage."

Mae Lee's daddy frowned and scratched his head when she eventually gave her carefully prepared speech about wanting to get married. She made her daddy chuckle when she mentioned she'd be helping win the war, reminding him of her young friends who had already married. But then her daddy grew serious. "Right now, you need to set your mind on graduating from high school." He looked his young daughter in the eye. "Are you sure you're not wanting to get married so you'll get some of those allotment checks?"

Mae Lee's eyes widened. "Checks, what checks? Do they pay you to marry a soldier, Daddy?"

"You are so young, my child." Her daddy shook his head. "Now, suppose you bring this young man over to see me."

Mae Lee pushed her mouth into a pretty pout. "Daddy, you've seen him every Sunday since I turned sixteen and a half."

"This time I mean for him to *see* me," her daddy said.

For five Sundays straight Mae Lee waited for Jeff Barnes

to come. She especially wanted him to see that they had just had electric lights put in. From the time the Rural Electrification Administration started running power lines throughout the farming areas, Mae Lee's mama had longed for electricity. And after a few months' work at the munitions plant she had saved enough to help pay to have the power lines brought to their farmhouse.

The first night the electric lights were turned on, Mae Lee stood outside looking at the brightly lighted house until her mama made her come inside and go to bed. Even if it would be broad daylight and the sun shining when Jeff Barnes came to visit, Mae Lee knew she would turn on the electric lamp with the eggshell lampshade in the tiny company room.

On the day that Jeff Barnes was due to come, Mae Lee knew it would be afternoon before he arrived, but she started dressing early in the morning. She put on her single pair of silk stockings, licking her fingers to soften away any rough edges as she carefully pulled them on, making sure the seams were straight. She didn't want to get a run in her only pair, then be forced to wear the honey-beige ribbed cotton-rayon stockings. She hated them. She left the top button undone on the lace Peter Pan collar of the rose-colored butcher-linen dress her mama had ordered from a National Bellas Hess catalog, so that a peek of her light golden skin showed. A little of the lace on her slip showed from under her dress, but that didn't bother her. The pink slip was a fine one. It was silk. Her mama bought good underthings.

After church services one Sunday, a gust of wind had blown

the preacher's wife's new crepe dress up and the words "Not For Sale" on the back of her homemade petticoat flashed in the full view of onlookers. No bleach or lye wash in the world could take out the lettering on the white cotton government flour bag. After that Mae Lee and her mama never wore a homemade petticoat again.

Mae Lee scrubbed her even-set teeth with Arm & Hammer baking soda mixed with a little salt until they glistened, nibbled on fresh sprigs of mint to freshen her breath, and waited.

When Jeff Barnes came, he was in a uniform. He was so good-looking. She thought she'd die if she couldn't marry him.

Under the watchful eyes of her father he sat on the davenport as close to her as it was proper, stealing occasional glances at her until it was time to leave.

The day they were married down at the county courthouse, Mae Lee was determined not to notice that while her mama grinned broadly, her father didn't smile once. All she could see and care about was the handsome young soldier at her side.

The young couple spent their wedding night in Jeff Barnes's mama's company bedroom. Mae Lee put the small valise her mama had packed for her under the four-poster bed. She ran her fingers across the pretty cotton chenille bedspread. "This is mighty pretty," she said, her voice shaking. Her new husband grinned. "So are you, Mae Lee."

The next day Mae Lee stood alongside the highway waiting for the Greyhound bus with her new husband, tall and proud. She wore the same outfit that she had been married in, a soft powder blue suit with matching blue ribbon streamers on her white straw hat. Her long brown hair was swept under in a pageboy style that framed her light golden skin and wide-set eyes. Her soft chin was determinedly set to be cheerful as she clung to the tall, handsome young man's arm.

Mae Lee was glad that the bus came quickly. She struggled for something to say, and so did he. Her husband kissed her good-bye and boarded the bus. She waved good-bye until the bus disappeared from her view, then removed the hat and picked up her valise. With her straw hat in her hand she walked home to her parents' house.

: 3 :

With husbands, sons, and even some daughters away at war, many farmers were forced to let their crops go. In some rural communities, it was almost as if nobody lived there anymore.

Mae Lee's daddy was determined not to let the crabgrass and jimsonweeds overtake his cotton crop, and, as in the year before, he had his daughter's help. Only now there was more farm work to do. His newly married daughter had insisted on her own additional farm crops. She had talked with her father long into the night about the best cash crops to plant. When she decided she would also farm sweet potatoes and peanuts in addition to her few acres of cotton, her daddy forewarned she'd have a hard time with the hoeing to keep the grass out of all those crops.

In the early spring, with her daddy's help, she'd bedded her seed sweet potatoes for plants and had plants ready to transplant into the fields as soon as they had late spring and early summer rains.

While his daughter hoed, Sam Hudson plowed. He worked his mule Maude in the morning, Molly in the afternoon. When he caught up with the plowing, he helped his daughter. They hoed from early dawn to sundown, stopping only for a noon-day dinner break to eat the food that Vergie Hudson cooked before going to her job in the munitions plant. At day's end, Mae Lee would milk Starlight and help her daddy feed and water the livestock.

Mae Lee was always sure to be home around noontime. That was when the mailman usually arrived. Every day for almost a month she'd rushed to the mailbox hoping there would be a letter, a postcard, some word from her husband. After the first postcard giving her his address, there was nothing. Her heart always began to race when she saw the mailman's car, barely visible in a cloud of dust, rounding the curve on the dry dirt road. As he slowed to a stop she closed her eyes against the dust that surrounded her.

"Got some important mail today," the mailman called out. Her heart leaped. Her eyes registered her happiness.

"It's your application for ration book number three," he said and handed her a brownish yellow envelope.

Mae Lee's heart sank. Just another book filled with page after page of ration stamps, printed with pictures of fighter planes, aircraft carriers, army tanks, howitzers, and then pages of numbered and lettered ration stamps. Stamps allowing them to buy foods they couldn't afford in the first place. To families like hers they didn't need to say, "Give your whole support to rationing and thereby conserve our vital goods. If you don't need it, DON'T BUY IT."

The heat had gotten to her that day, and rushing to the mailbox hadn't helped. The world swirled around her. Mr. Wesley, the mailman, was only a blur. He reached for the envelope in her hand, and read from it as if she could not read. True, at the time she couldn't.

"This application must be mailed between June 1 and June 10, 1943. Applications will not be accepted after August 1. Affix postage before mailing."

He turned the form over and read on. "It's only two cents postage if it's mailed in Charlotte, North Carolina, but from here it will be three cents. Now remember, Mae Lee, you are not in Charlotte, North Carolina. You are in South Carolina. If y'all need stamps, put your pennies in the mailbox and I'll put them on."

Mae Lee's daddy saw her slump by the mailbox. He rushed to help her inside the house. He was worried. "I must find somebody to work in your place, Mae Lee. You've got to stop working in the hot sun. It's too hot out there. I'm going to try and get you on at the munitions plant where your mama works. If you are not with child. Are you?"

Mae Lee wasn't. She got a job at the plant. She worked her shifts and wrote letters to her husband. It hurt that he didn't answer, but she wrote him anyway. She wrote about everything from old man Cooper's bout with lumbago to radio announcer Grady Cole's new slant on Hadacol, "the cure-all bottled remedy." Some folks said the true name should have been "alcohol remedy." And in every letter she sent a folded piece of white paper with blotted kisses of love in the ever-popular blackberry shade of lipstick. Her letters always ended with "Forever yours." She didn't scold him for not writing. If he happened not to make it through, she didn't want him to die angry with her. She never mentioned that she was working or saving to buy a piece of land. Their land. That was going to be the big surprise.

She stayed on with her mama and daddy, sleeping in the same cramped bedroom she had slept in as a child. When and if her husband came home from the war for good, she wanted them to move into their very own house on their own land.

The work at the munitions plant was hard. Hardest of all was changing shifts. There were three shifts. The first was from 7:00 a.m. to 3:00 p.m., the second from 3:00 p.m. to 11:00 p.m., and the third from 11:00 p.m. to 7:00 a.m. Mae Lee would work one of the day shifts for two weeks then switch to the next shift for two weeks. Sometimes she worked in the paint division, painting shells. She stood on her feet during all her hours of work, but the pay was good.

Every payday after work she pulled out a small tin bucket with a thin wire handle, pried open the recessed lid, and put her money inside. Her daddy had bought the little bucket for her; he called it her money safe.

Mae Lee saved almost every penny she earned. The few pieces of clothing she bought were all black, just in case. Over and over the radio told about the soldiers killed in the war. If anything should happen to Jeff, she believed she would wear black mourning clothes for as long as she lived.

One day in midsummer Mae Lee had time off from work. Her daddy had finished the final plowing for all his crops and didn't need her help. She went over to visit her friend Ella-belle. As they sat chatting out on the porch, a car drove up.

It was painted olive drab, the army color. Mae Lee got up to leave, but Ellabelle begged her to stay. "You never know what they might be up to," she whispered.

They watched the two men start up the narrow path to the little house. One of them carried a briefcase.

"Ellabelle Ellis?"

"Yes, sir, that's me." Ellabelle stood up.

The officer spoke in soft tones, his face drawn with traces of sadness, yet official and stern. "We have a telegram for you," he said.

Ellabelle started shaking her head as he read, "We regret to inform you that your husband, Will Leroy Ellis, a rifleman in the Forty-fourth Infantry Division, has been killed in action."

The officers helped Ellabelle inside her house after she slumped to the floor. Mae Lee watched, speechless and helpless. How many messages had they delivered like that one? If her own husband realized how much she needed to hear from him to be assured he was safe, then surely he would write.

After Ellabelle received her husband's GI insurance check from the army, she and her parents moved away. As much as Mae Lee hated to see them go, the thoughts of the house they left, and the farmland the Grangers might be persuaded to sell along with it, helped ease the loneliness.

Late one Saturday night in the spring of 1945, Mae Lee and her parents took the money she had saved and spread it out on the kitchen table to count. Mae Lee's daddy broke into a joyous laugh. "My baby girl has a few thousand dollars here.

I'm going to see Mr. Granger about that land and empty house on the hill first thing Monday morning. There is way more than twenty acres there."

Mae Lee was anxious and worried. "Maybe he might not even want to sell it."

"Oh, he'll let us buy it, since it's near to the land he sold your mama years ago. He probably won't even ask too much for it. Only about ten acres or so right alongside the road is decent farmland. Most of the ground all along Catfish Creek is bottomland, too wet for cotton, but, oh Lord, it'll grow sugarcane and late corn."

Sam Hudson pulled a cotton drawstring tobacco pouch from his pocket and emptied its contents on the table. Mae Lee stared at the pile of carefully folded money. "It's your share of the cotton crop, honey. Without your help the grass would have eaten it up." Her mama added a small wad of crumpled bills. "Since I didn't help this year, I'm giving you the share your daddy gave me," she said. "Now you and your husband will have a little farm to start out with."

The morning the papers were to be signed, Mae Lee was up early. When she got to the kitchen she was surprised to see that her daddy wasn't dressed and ready to go with her to buy the property. He was in his work clothes sitting at the table and drinking coffee.

"I guess you wouldn't want to wear your Sunday suit on a weekday, Daddy, but it seems like you would at least wear a white shirt and necktie and the clean, creased overalls Mama starched and ironed," his daughter said. She glanced nervously at the clock. "Oh," she said, "we have plenty of time. I got ready early, I was afraid I'd be late. It's over an hour before nine o'clock."

Her daddy made some makeshift excuse that the gout was settling in on his big toe again, and he needed to use what little strength he had to string his newly planted watermelon patch. The old crows had made friends with the scarecrow he put up and, row by row, were digging up and eating his watermelon seeds, he said. "Besides," he added, "you ended up not needing me after all to get that paying job of yours over at the munitions plant. You'll be able to handle this land deal; you will be fine."

Mae Lee was near tears. "But, Daddy, Mr. Jay Granger's not just another white man. This is big business. I won't know how to deal with him."

Her daddy set his coffee cup down and slapped his hand against the table. "I clean forgot to tell you, you won't be dealing with Jay Granger. He and Mrs. Granger's moving to Florida. He's turned everything over to his son Church. You'll get a fair deal from Church Granger; can't say he's a chip off the old block."

Sam Hudson got up to pour another cup of coffee. His face grew serious. "Let me tell you, child, if it was Jay Granger you were dealing with, I'd be right there at your side. Jay Granger can find a way to cheat a dead man. I never will forget how he tried to cheat poor old Jonah Walker out of his entire cotton crop one year, a full year's work. Down to this day I do believe that Jay Granger still thinks he cheated old Jonah that year." A pleased grin crossed her daddy's face. He leaned back in his chair, his coffee cup cradled in his hands. He loved to tell a good story.

"It had been almost time for the county fair. I was loading up a bale of cotton on my old pickup to take to the cotton gin when Jonah Walker hurried across the cotton field. He pulled a crumpled paper poke from under his arm. He pointed to a pint glass jar inside. 'Want a little nip?' I shook my head. 'What's the trouble, Jonah?' I said.

"Jonah's hand was trembling, but he held on to his jar. 'I went over to Mr. Jay Granger's this morning to check out with him. My wife was after me to start handing her a little piece of money to start buying the winter shoes and clothes for the children. She'd tried to buy a bolt of cotton flannel down at the general store on time but old man Falls say he didn't like to give credit when the cotton season was about over.

" 'Well,' he continued, 'Mr. Granger commenced a-figuring. After a long time he looked at me, took a long draw on his hand-rolled Prince Albert cigarette and leaned back in his chair. He blew smoke into the air.' Jonah leaned close to me, too close, his stale moonshine breath right in my face. 'I swear, Sam,' he said, 'every puff of smoke old man Granger blew formed a ring, every single time.' I held my breath and stepped back.

"Jonah went on. ' "Jonah," Mr. Granger says to me, "seems like we got bad news. From what I figure, and I've never been wrong as I know of, it's going to take you a few more bales of cotton, and even then I won't promise you that you'll break even with your debts this year." '

"Jonah wiped his eyes with the back of his hand. ' "Mr.

Granger," I said, "how much do you figure I'll end up getting?" He sat there and flicked small pieces of tobacco from his rolled cigarette off his tongue. "Nothing, Jonah. Nothing. Maybe next year will be better." '

"Jonah's voice choked. He wiped his eyes again. He was crying. 'I tried to tell him he was wrong, Sam. That my cotton crop had been the best I'd ever had, but he out-figured me. He just plumb out-figured me.'

"Then he leaned against the truck fender and unscrewed the lid off the little jar and took a nip. Then a few swallows. He turned the jar to its side. He tilted his head to look at the white lightning that was still left. 'At least I have a corner left,' he said. Then a short time later he brightened. 'I've got a plan in my head that I think will put shoes and clothes on my children and something on the table for the winter.' His voice dropped to a tremor, and he peeped up at me shyly. 'Mr. Granger may out-figure me on paper but there is no way a white man who ain't never picked a boll of cotton in his life can out-figure me in the cotton field. I can skim off a couple of light bales of cotton and he'll never know it.' Then Jonah looked at me. 'But I can't do it without you, Sam. Since you own your land, with your help we can pull it off.'

"And so Jonah picked two sacks of cotton for the master and one for his family. Jonah hid the cotton in the woods for me to pick up at night. And when there was enough for a bale I took the cotton to the gin. Jay Granger's gin, mind you," he chuckled, "and had the cotton ginned for my own. Let me tell you, Mae Lee, even half full of moonshine and tipsy, Jonah Walker could outwit most of the white people in Rising Ridge, South Carolina."

When her daddy told her that he had already talked over the land deal with Church Granger, she felt better. All that was needed now was her signature and the money. A pleased grin spread over her daddy's face when she put on her new navy straw hat with red cherries and stood before him for his approval. "Mama said, 'A real businesswoman always wears a hat,'" she said. Her daddy shook his head. "You are so much like your mama," he said. "Now, little girl, you are sure you have all the money we counted out again last night? Sure you didn't ease a little of it out of the paper poke?"

Mae Lee laughed. "I did take a little," she teased, taking her daddy's straw hat off his head and putting it back on. "Took one penny and I need it back. Bet you a penny you'll touch your hat?"

"Bet you a penny I won't."

Then, as always, in their old childhood game, he reached and adjusted his hat. His daughter collected and left.

Church Granger had asked her to come to his house, so she took the shortcut through the woods, then headed up the road toward the big house.

She didn't notice the mud on her shoes until she was almost up to his front porch. Why hadn't she taken the long way there, along the hard-surfaced highway? But maybe it was good she hadn't. Her new hat might have been blown off by a passing big truck and crushed under its wheels.

After she had wiped her shoes as clean as she could on the lawn, she made her way to the front door. She knocked, then stepped back from the door to wait. It was shady on the long, wide porch, with its huge columns and white wicker chairs. It was the finest house in the whole world.

It struck her that maybe she should have gone to the back door. She knew Lula Jane would have gone to the back door. But that's where the kitchen was, and Lula Jane would have been coming to cook. She was here for business, to buy land. She was dressed up in silk stockings and a hat. Mae Lee smoothed the edges of her brown hair swept up in a pompadour. Men respected women in hats. She stood tall and straight. She deserved respect, she thought to herself. She painted gun shells at the munitions plant.

Church Granger answered the door. "Hey, Mae Lee," he said. He led her into a room off the long hallway. A quick glance at the desk in the book-lined room made her think his wife, Liddie, had just left the room. On the desk, a gold-rimmed cup with a matching saucer was half-filled with tea. Roses in a heavy white flowered vase had been cut by some-one that morning. It was surely Liddie Granger's desk. Mae Lee imagined she was upstairs getting dressed to go out. A clock, with pale flowers in the center of the face, stood in a glass case. Old books in washed out maroons, reds, and grays, with deep-rose satin ribbons hanging out of them, were stacked here and there on the desk. A bundle of letters tied with matching ribbons lay on top of one stack, near a beau-tiful white feather pen and a fancy inkwell. A speckled, dark blue fountain pen trimmed in gold lay across an unfinished letter—a letter that Mae Lee thought had to be in a woman's handwriting. There was no way a man could write that fancy. Mae Lee's eyes slid around the room. She wanted to have the good manners not to stare, but couldn't help it when there was that portrait staring down at her, the face looking like some man who'd had his land given to him by land grant, she thought. Hanging there over the high carved mantlepiece, he looked out at the rows of richly colored books, the wide-back chairs, and the big table that was polished to such a high shine that it reflected the stained-glass colors of the tall reading lamp like a mirror. Mae Lee wanted to take in every detail so she'd never forget it.

She had stared so long and hard at the desk she hadn't noticed that there was someone else in the room. A well-dressed man was standing by the long, fabric-draped window near the corner of the room. She didn't know him. She was uncomfortable. When she'd passed a mirror in the entrance hall, she noticed that her hat was a little crooked. Her hat pin had worked loose, but she was too embarrassed to try and pin it, so she left it alone.

At Church's invitation to sit down, Mae Lee perched on the seat edge of a big wine-colored leather armchair and crossed her ankles. Mae Lee was more nervous than she'd ever been in her life. Liddie came in to say good-bye to her husband. She brightened when she saw Mae Lee and apologized to her for having to leave. Mae Lee felt briefly reassured by her warmth, but then Liddie left the room.

Church Granger didn't seem in any hurry. He talked with the man by the window about cotton and cottonseed oil before turning to her.

"This young lady wants to buy some land," he announced half-jokingly.

"Yes, sir, I do," she confirmed in a serious voice.

Church Granger grew serious too. "Save for just a little over ten acres alongside that back road, most of the land is bottom-land." He eyed her closely. "Guess you didn't know that, did you, Mae Lee?"

She thought about how her daddy would have answered, what he would have said. "Always remember," her daddy had said, "they will never sell you their best, so take what you can get and make it good." So she just sat there with her eyes glued to the floor, studying the pattern in the rug.

Mae Lee glanced up at Church Granger. He was steadily writing something down on paper. Maybe what he was doing was trying to out-figure her on the land. Thinking of Jonah Walker made her lift her eyes and stare straight at him. Maybe he was like his daddy, after all. But working at the plant had changed her. One of the head men over at the plant had said he knew he could always trust Mae Lee Barnes's count on everything. So Church wasn't going to be able to out-figure her. She and her daddy had figured and counted the money most of the night. Now she held on to her pocketbook with both hands, wishing her daddy was there with her.

Church Granger stood up and walked toward her chair. "If everything here looks agreeable to you, Mae Lee, Mr. Rayford will witness your signature." He handed her some papers and a fountain pen. Mae Lee read through the papers carefully and allowed herself a small inner smile when she saw the final fig-ures. This was really going to be her home and her land with the help of her parents.

When she piled the money on the desk, a startled but pleased looked crossed Church Granger's face. "That looks like a pretty big sum of money, Mae Lee."

"It's all there, sir. Every penny of it."

He flashed a grin. "Now, you are sure you don't want to wait for your husband to come home from the war to do this?"

"I'm sure," Mae Lee said. "I want it to be a surprise. A real big surprise."

: 4 :

Jeff Barnes returned from the war without a scratch. Mae Lee was in the kitchen washing her hair when she heard someone knock. She wrapped a towel around her head and answered the door, and there he stood, with his duffel bag slung over his shoulder, smiling down at her. His handsome face was stronger now, but he still had his easy, boyish grin. He was so clean and trim in his crisp uniform, he was so perfect, even more handsome than she'd remembered. She started to cry. Her husband put his duffel bag down and pulled her into his arms covering her face with kisses, saying, "Don't cry, baby, I'm here, I'm home. We've got a lot of catching up to do." He pulled an arm free and picked up his duffel. "I need to get unpacked. Are we staying here tonight?"

Mae Lee smiled. Her eyes glistened through the tears. She wiped her eyes, and looked up at Jeff. "We won't have to stay at anyone's house tonight. We'll be staying in the little house above Catfish Creek. The Jenkins family moved out months ago. Mama and Daddy helped me get the house all fixed up. It's ready for us to move in."

Jeff Barnes's face broke into a wide grin. "That's great, baby." He pulled her close and kissed her again. "I wouldn't mind sleeping on a pallet on the floor with you tonight."

Through the open bedroom door, he watched Mae Lee get her things together and move from his view to change her dress. When she stepped into the doorway she had combed her still damp hair and put on natural Tangee lipstick.

"You're still pretty, Mae Lee," he grinned. Then his face eased into a frown. "I guess I'll be able to stay on at Jay Granger's place. But the man isn't Rising Ridge's best land-owner. The war changes a man, baby, changes the way he thinks." He shrugged his shoulders. "It's good farming land. I guess I can tolerate Jay Granger until we can get on our feet."

A warm feeling of satisfaction swept over Mae Lee. "The house isn't on Jay Granger's land."

"He died?"

"No, he's still alive."

"I guess he started turning things over to his son after the war?"

Mae Lee dug her fingernails into the palms of her hands and clenched her teeth to keep from telling him that they now owned not only the house but all the land that the Jenkinses had farmed as sharecroppers. She wanted to tell him it was theirs free and clear. But the time to tell him wasn't right. She would know when it was. Every woman knows the time to tell really good news, she thought. At the proper time she would tell him everything from start to finish.

The proper time to tell her good news was a few seconds later—the time that it took to pull the shoebox with the land deed in it from beneath her bed.

Jeff Barnes was overwhelmed. He kept shaking his head, "I can't believe it! Now I know why I love you so much. I knew that you were special when I told you that the name Barnes suited you better than Hudson."

Nine months and four days after Mae Lee's husband returned from the war their first daughter, Dallace, was born.

As much as it had pleased Jeff Barnes to have his own land to farm, it was not enough to hold him there in Rising Ridge. Once the season's harvest was over, he left home to look for work in a nearby city. Mae Lee blamed the war. It was the war, she decided, that dried up all his interest in farming. But at least he had tried, she thought to herself. His first year back on the farm was a failure. It had rained so much during the growing season, the crops were sometimes underwater for days. And, of course, she blamed herself. She felt she had been of little help. Instead of going away, the first month's morning sickness hung on, stretched into day sickness, and kept up throughout her pregnancy.

Mercifully, her daddy was able to get his longtime friend Hooker Jones and his wife Maycie to farm the land for her on shares. Hooker Jones had moved from a big landowner's farm after a heated dispute over a few bales of cotton. They were getting older, so the smaller farm suited them well.

Jeff Barnes planted a tree the day their son, Taylor, was born. It was one of the rare occasions of his presence whose date she could later pinpoint exactly. It was not as easy to pinpoint the planting of the seeds for her three other children, Annie Ruth, Nellie Grace, and Amberlee. Four years went by during which time Mae Lee gave birth to four children. Three girls and one boy. Jeff would come home for a few weeks, she would conceive a child, and then he would be off again. He never announced when he was coming, he just showed up. If he was earning a decent salary where he worked, it almost never took the form of bringing money home. Mae Lee knew that her parents were disgusted with her husband's failure to provide or to help on the farm, but they said nothing to her, and she made a point of never expressing even the slightest impatience or dissatisfaction with him in their presence. Eventually, she told herself, Jeff would settle down with his family for good. After his years in the army he was restless, that was all. For now, she only knew his pattern. He would come home, and then after a few weeks announce that he'd heard of a better job someplace else, and would look all lovesick at her with his strange-colored eyes and say, "Baby, we are going to have to move on. I won't go without you. I absolutely refuse." And each time he'd stand there waiting for her answer, knowing full well she wouldn't go. As in times past, she would only look at him and hold her body stiff, aware that while he might be leaving, a very real part of him remained with her, his newly conceived child.

After their youngest child, Amberlee, was born and she'd survived a few visits from him without getting pregnant again, the next time he offered to take her with him she took him up on it. She meant it, and was so excited by her decision that she misread the pained disappointment in her husband's eyes, the crack in his voice, as signs of his surprise and pleasure.

She ran to her parents' house to tell them about leaving with her husband. Jeff had only one room in the town where he lived, so they thought it would be best to take only the baby until they found a house. She turned to her daddy, her face took on a soft glow, her eyes danced with delight. "I know you won't like the idea of our renting, when the same money could be buying, Daddy, but it's what my husband wants to do. You have my word, though, we'll hold on to our land."

Her daddy frowned. "Talk is easy, baby girl, very easy." Mae Lee hadn't heard. She turned to her mama. "Mama, I hope it's not asking too much of you to take care of the older ones until we can come back for them. It won't be for long. Just make them behave, Mama. They won't be too much trouble. You know they'll mind you."

Vergie Hudson looked out her window at her grandchildren playing in the yard and smiled. "I have them at my house all day even when you are home, Mae Lee. But maybe you do need to write out some instructions for me on how to care for my grands." She grew serious when her daughter broke into laughter. "Just don't move too fast with that husband of yours. Take a little time to sort things out."

"I've got to move fast," Mae Lee put in. "We'll be leaving in a few days. Just think, Mama, I'll be living in town. Living like a lady. Jeff said he was going to send me to the beauty shop. 'All the women in town go,' he said."

The next few days Mae Lee was up early, washing and ironing and baking sweet goodies for her children. They were as excited over moving to their grandparents' as she was over her move to town.

Dallace, her oldest, watched as Mae Lee ran a hot iron over a small bunch of cedar tree branches piled on the makeshift ironing board. Mae Lee explained that the cedar branches not only cleared away sticky starch from the iron, it also made the clothes smell good.

On the day they were to leave, her husband worked outside on his old car, fixing something under the hood, while she dressed. Mae Lee packed what she felt was her best, and searched through her old dresser drawers for a piece of taffeta ribbon to try and anchor a bow in her baby's few strands of hair. "We want Daddy to let people see his baby is a little girl."

Mae Lee heard Jeff's car crank up. "Come, baby," she said, wedging a soft little foot into a freshly polished white shoe, "Daddy's waiting for us."

She paused to look in a smoke-stained mirror with splotches of peeling in the back. She turned her head until she could see her face, adjusted her navy straw hat with the red plastic cherries to just the right angle. And with baby in one arm, a suitcase closed and tied with a leather belt in the other, she turned for a final look in the mirror.

She no longer heard the car running and she guessed Jeff had only started it to make sure it would crank, and was coming inside for her.

She heard footsteps on the porch. "Jeff," she called out, "come and get the suitcase. We have to stop by Mama's. I forgot and left the new baby blankets down there."

Her mama's image, not Jeff's, appeared in the mirror. "What

ails you, child?" Her mama frowned. "Talking to yourself like some addle-minded woman." She didn't wait for her daughter to answer. "Guess I'd be a little 'off' too if I had to put up with the likes of Jeff Barnes."

Mae Lee held her baby close. "Mama, he's taking us with him this time. We'll be back for the children as soon as we can get settled. I promise. They won't be too much trouble. You know they are good children."

Vergie Hudson sat on the foot of the iron-poster bed. She hugged her arms tightly across her chest and pulled her mouth in at the corners. She always did that when she was making serious talk.

"Go see for yourself," she said quietly, then moved quickly to take her grandbaby from her daughter's arms. Mae Lee did not move.

Her mama relaxed the tightness of her lips. She cradled the baby's pretty, perfectly shaped head in both hands. "We've shaped it just right," she said, as if she'd ever allowed her daughter to dare touch the baby's head. All Mae Lee had been told to do was to turn the baby every so often when it lay in its little homemade crib, and never to drop it.

"Well, anyway," she went on, "your daddy just happened to glance out the window and saw Jeff turning his car around in the front yard. He didn't think a thing till he turned it off and started pushing it, then jumped in and let it coast down the hill. Then, hold the lamb, the fool cranked the car up and took off like the devil chasing lightning. Your poor daddy shook his head. 'That snake in the grass is slipping off from my baby girl,' he said. 'He is leaving her. And I'll bet my baby don't even suspect, don't even suspect.'" Mae Lee's mama licked her lips and rubbed her pointing finger across them. "Now, what do you have to say to that?"

"Jeff's probably gone to buy some gas, Mama."

Mae Lee's mama shook her head, "Honey, honey. At the end of the dirt road is the highway. If you turn right you're headed north, if you turn left you're headed south to town. The gas station's in town. Jeff Barnes was heading north."

Mae Lee didn't turn to face her mama; she just closed her eyes and gave herself a good personal silent cussing out. To think, she told herself, that I actually prayed, prayed day and night, for him to return alive from the war.

She stood there, her eyes fixed on her own image in the mirror, a grown woman with tears making paths down through a layer of Sweet Georgia Brown face powder, crying when no one was dead. A grown woman crying over a man who no longer wanted her. She made no effort to straighten her navy straw hat, terribly crooked on her head because of her baby's attempts to reach the red cherries.

She wanted to run beyond the small branch of water just below her house to the banks of the big river and throw herself into the flowing waters. She wanted to scream out to her mama to leave. But she stood and listened, ashamed to turn and face her mama, forgetting that the mirror fully revealed her intense pain and shame.

Her mama laid her grandbaby on the bed and stood beside Mae Lee. She looked at her daughter's tear-streaked face in the mirror. She wanted to take her child in her arms and comfort her, but Mae Lee's eyes told her no. It was the time for both of them to be strong.

Her mama started pulling her mouth in at the corners again.

"I tried to warn you about that Barnes boy," she fussed. She hadn't, but Mae Lee was not about to say so. You don't tell your mama to her face what she did or didn't say, not even when you are old enough to be a mama yourself. Not even when you know for a fact she didn't say it.

"You were not the only one. There was your friend, Doris Ann. Her mama tried to tell her about them Barnes boys, too. But no, you both wouldn't listen. Good-looking boys with eyes that light color, a high-brown complexion and good hair on their head don't spell nothing but trouble. Everybody knows it. Everybody but young girls who won't listen to their mamas and go fool crazy over them. You know what happened to Doris Ann—well, it's happened to you."

Mae Lee wanted to remind her mama that she didn't exactly have dark eyes, either. White folks called Mae Lee's eyes hazel. At least that's what the woman put on her job application. But still she said nothing. You didn't talk back to your mama. A daughter wasn't supposed to.

Mae Lee watched her mama in the mirror. The cracked mirror gave extra anger lines to her mama's face, already blown up with contempt. She wondered what her mama would have done if her daughter'd been like a certain war bride down the road. With a husband away at war, there she was, stealing every forbidden moment she could to be with one of the handsome young German POW's brought in by the hundreds to harvest seasonal crops. Now, you talk about strange-colored eyes. It was a good thing the girl's mama hurried up and got her out of Rising Ridge. No telling what color of eyes the baby that girl was expecting would end up with. If that had been her—her mama would have had something to see. She would have died.

Vergie observed her daughter lost in thought and eyed her suspiciously.

"Is there another young'un on the way?"

"No, ma'am. I don't think so."

"Well, there is one on the way. You'll find out soon enough."

"Oh, Mama, do you really think I'm pregnant again?"

Her mama raised her eyes upward. "Why certainly. You married a Barnes, didn't you?" She turned to look at her sleeping grandbaby. She shook her head. "But, oh Lord, them Barnes boys do make pretty babies."

Mae Lee started undressing her baby girl. Her tears still flowed. She cried not for him but for herself. Nobody used Mae Lee. "The war changed him," she said slowly. "It was the war, Mama. After the war, Mama, there was this new way about him. I could never get used to it. He was always on the move. Always in a rush to go someplace. He was shell-shocked. And you know what that will do to any able-bodied man."

It had not all been bad. There had been times when things were good between them, warm and easy, like well-worn soft leather gloves. And there were her babies. Five healthy, beautiful children.

Vergie Hudson looked about her daughter's small room. She fingered the fringed dresser scarf and looked at the fancy pincushions, the round, cardboard Coty dusting powder box, the comb, brush, and mirror dresser set, and the blue bottle of Evening in Paris perfume. "Your husband may not have written you letters but he sure was thinking about you. He bought you some right nice presents," she said.

Mae Lee's voice quivered, she was crying again. "He said he did write letters to me, Mama, but his spelling was so bad he was ashamed to mail them, so he tore the letters up."

"Huh," her mama grunted, "like you couldn't have made out what he was trying to say. I wish he'd have mailed them. Oh, how my heart ached for you."

"Jeff has been shell-shocked, Mama," she repeated. That was safe. Mae Lee didn't tell her mother that during all the years Jeff Barnes was in the army he had never left the supply department where he sewed on buttons and rank stripes. And that she, not her husband, had bought those things.

Mae Lee's mama started to moan softly. She moved to her daughter's side and put her arms around her daughter, patting and rubbing her back as if she were a baby needing to be burped. "He'll come back, baby," her mother soothed. "He will come back to his little sweet family."

Mae Lee pulled away. She no longer cried. "Maybe he will come back, Mama, but he will *never* come back to me," she said firmly. She took her hat off and pulled her long hair into a braid. "The first thing I'll do tomorrow is ask Daddy to put new locks on the doors. I don't ever want to see Jeff Barnes again in this life."

The next morning, Mae Lee's daddy changed the locks, and said flat out, "Get yourself dressed, young lady, we're going down to lawyer Gaines's office to see about getting you a divorce. He'll know where you have to go and what you have to do to make it legal. You don't need the likes of one of them Barneses trailing in and out for the rest of your life."

Mae Lee gave herself six months to get over her husband. Six months to grieve inwardly and be sad. After that it was finished.

Part : II

: 5 :

Even with the help from Hooker Jones and his wife Maycie, keeping the farm going wasn't easy for Mae Lee. Hooker's wife was in poor health. And, although she rarely complained, so was Mae Lee's mama. She had kidney trouble. Yet she was always there, helping out on the farm and with the grandchildren.

"The farm is too much for you," Mae Lee's mama would moan. "You need help. To be married. Besides," she'd add, "you've got the hip set for more babies." Then she would hint. "I don't reckon you'd fuss too much if Howard Jamison would drop by for a few minutes or so Sunday. It's been a while since that wife of his died. He'd make some lucky woman a mighty good husband."

Then her mama would look at her hard. "You need to start wearing your straw hat more and protect your smooth, light skin and get some rest. A man's not going to want some woman that's worn herself to a frazzle. As soon as we get caught up with our hoeing, I'll come and help you out with yours."

Every time her mama had come to help, however, there had always been someone there to pull her away. On one occasion, after it had rained for days and the grass was about to take over Mae Lee's cotton crop and poor Maycie was sick, her mama left off her own hoeing and came over to help.

Just then, who drove up in her fine car but Liddie Granger, Church's wife. "Don't look up, Mama," Mae Lee urged, but her mama had already stood her hoe up and was walking over to the car.

Liddie Granger leaned over and rolled down the car window on the passenger side. Mae Lee could hear a baby crying. Liddie sounded as if she was crying too, "Vergie, Vergie, my baby is crying and I can't get him to stop. My mama is away. Oh, Vergie, please help me. I don't know what to do. I really don't."

Vergie looked over her shoulder at her daughter leaning on her hoe. "Go on, Mama," waved Mae Lee.

Vergie took off her shoes, knocked them together several times to shake off the soft dirt, and got into Liddie Granger's car. Mae Lee watched them leave with the crying baby. What a pair they made, Liddie Granger with every strand of hair in place, face powder on, and her mama barefoot, in old field clothes and a frizzed straw hat.

"If my baby was sick I don't think I'd take time to put all that stuff on my face," she thought, but shrugged it off. "She probably already had it on."

Mae Lee's daddy always said he'd never think too hard of the young Grangers. After all, they sold her the land she owned, something very few white landowners in Rising Ridge would do. He made her promise to hold on to it.

Watching the car disappear down the road, Mae Lee was jealous of the fine life Liddie Granger lived, terribly jealous. Liddie was so rich. In her jealousy she had forgotten all about her own children, happily playing in the shade from the trees at the edge of the woods. Mae Lee never ever carried her children into the cotton fields, because her mama always said, "If small children play up and down the cotton rows while their parents work, they will grow up to be cotton pickers. And if they pry open a green cotton boll with a boll weevil inside, they will have a short, tragic life." Her mama always spoke of her regrets over letting her play in the cotton fields while she worked. But Vergie Hudson had made sure Mae Lee would be so afraid of the boll weevil inside a green, unopened cotton boll, that she'd never pry one open.

It had been fine for her mama to tell her when she returned that Mrs. Granger's baby was all right. She'd gotten it to sleep. But when her mama kept on talking, Mae Lee hoed furiously. "Mama, I don't want to hear about the new things in that house, the presents her husband bought her, the good supper Lula Jane is cooking for her tonight," she said. "Why couldn't she take care of the baby?"

"Lula Jane don't know nothing about no children, look at how she messed up with hers. When it comes to mothering she is as bad as some cuckoo birds. Well anyway, as I was saying—" "Mama," she cut her short. "I don't believe I want to hear any more."

"Oh, good, then," her mama grinned, waving a crisp five

dollar bill in her hand. "I thought you wanted to hear how I was planning on splitting what I made on that little short trip."

Mae Lee threw her hoe down and chased her mama up and down the cotton rows.

The two women sat down at the edge of the field to rest. Vergie Hudson pulled sprouting grass from around the cotton plants on nearby rows. Her face grew serious. She looked across the field at Hooker and her husband plowing the land he loved so much. She listened to him calling out "gee," "haw" to the mules. She pulled a crumpled letter from her shirt pocket. "Your granddaddy's going down fast," she said. "Mama wrote and asked if I could come down and help out for a while. It'll be hard on your daddy for me to pull up and go down to the Low Country right in the middle of the farm season, but I'm going to have to go. You know, Mae Lee, that your grandma is in no better shape than your grandpa." Vergie had stopped short of saying that due to her own poor health it would be hard on her as well.

Mae Lee stood up and reached for her mama's hand. "I'll take care of Daddy," she promised. "You go and get Grandpa and Grandma ready to come to Rising Ridge so we both can take care of them."

The year was 1955. A troubling fear swept into the farmhouses, fanning out like a plague of bees, each family imagining their own stings. It was the year that Emmett Till was lynched in Mississippi. Mae Lee wept for him, just a young boy murdered in cold blood.

There was also a home problem she had to face. Her mama's

eyes had brimmed with tears when she told her that the day they'd feared had indeed finally come. She and Mae Lee's daddy had decided they were going to have to leave Rising Ridge and move to Low Country South Carolina to take care of her mama's aged sick parents, rather than the other way around. Her grandmother, a diabetic, was rapidly losing her eyesight, but she was still caring for her grandfather who had suffered a stroke. Vergie's efforts to get her parents to move to Up Country and live with her had failed. Her mother stubbornly refused to move. "We won't be taken from our home, not while we can lift a finger to hold on to the doorknob." And the children had to look out for the parents, even if it meant moving away to the Low Country. "Mae Lee, we will have to leave as soon as the fall harvest is finished," her mama said. "Your daddy's already made arrangements for Hooker Jones to farm his land on the halves. Hooker and his wife claim with you helping out so much, the three of you can run both farms. You and your children can move into our house, so they can live in yours."

Mae Lee and her parents finished the fall harvest early. The last bale of cotton was ginned two days before the November eleventh Veterans Day parade, a big event in Rising Ridge. Since most of the crops were harvested there was always a Christmas float included in the parade to get people in the buying spirit, with a Santa Claus tossing candies and small gifts into the crowds. On the day of the parade, dressed in warm mittens and tasseled knit caps, and under the watchful eyes of their mama and grandparents, Mae Lee's children eagerly scampered about gathering the goodies. Inside one of the stores, Mae Lee and her mama showed the children the pretty dolls and toys. The children wanted them all.

Before they left, Mae Lee's parents put all the Christmas presents they bought for the children under lock and key in the big chifforobe in their front company room. Mae Lee's mama reminded her over and over that she wouldn't be with her this time, so she mustn't forget to wrap the things they'd bought in the child's personal clothes. That way, even though they didn't have name tags, fancy wrappings, and bows, the children could tell which presents were theirs even before they could read. Vergie Hudson had already put the baseball she bought for Taylor in one of his socks, and wrapped a baby doll in Annie Ruth's little pink dress. She reminded her daughter of some of the good hiding places she used to search out on Christmas morning when she was a little girl. For Mae Lee's children, Christmas was like an Easter egg hunt.

A couple of days later Mae Lee's mama and daddy packed up the few things they were taking with them, and with help from a few neighbors, moved Mae Lee and her children from the little house she'd bought, back into the house where she had been born and grown up.

Mae Lee looked about the rooms, now crowded with her furniture as well as her mama's. She loved the new things her mama had. A Kelvinator, and an electric cooking stove and oil circulator to replace the potbellied wood-burning stove that had been in the kitchen. She step-measured enough space in a corner for Taylor's little bed, then measured with an outspread arm how much cretonne material it would take to run a drawstring curtain across. Poor little Taylor would still have to sleep in the kitchen, she thought. She looked at the nice front and back porches, but it was having a larger bedroom for her daughters that pleased her most.

It was late in the day before her parents were ready for departure. They hated to leave fully as much as she hated to see them go. Her mama reminded Mae Lee once again that her cousin Warren would always be there for her to go to in case of need. "Remember, Warren is a porter on the Southerner," she said, as if Mae Lee didn't know that very well, "so he can hold true to his promise that there'll always be food and a place at his table for you and my grandchildren. Warren will see that the family sticks together."

Her parents urged their grandchildren to be good, and showered them with candy, little gifts, hugs and kisses, which seemed to take away their sadness. Mae Lee fought to hold back tears. For her, there was no comfort.

Outside, before he climbed into his truck, her daddy put his hands on her shoulders. She dropped her head. "I'll do my best to keep things going until you all get back, Daddy," she said softly.

"Oh, you'll keep things going, Mae Lee. Just remember you are not going to be alone," he said. "You'll have help."

After they waved good-bye, Mae Lee's children went back inside the house, but she stayed out alone under the dreary fall sky. She thought of her daddy's parting words, "You'll have help." She wondered if some surprise awaited her, if there was something her daddy knew that she didn't. Maybe her husband was going to come back home. Perhaps her daddy felt that it might no longer matter to her what people might say if she took him back. She had been a grass widow too long, faced too many lonely nights alone in her marriage bed.

The feelings and desires for her husband that she thought were dead and buried were briefly very much alive, she realized, springing back like drought-parched corn coming back to life after soaking rains.

She felt the evening chill, and turned to go inside.

It was early on a cold winter day when Mae Lee's cousin Warren came by. Mae Lee had already started cooking. "It's too cold to do anything but eat," she said.

"And keep warm," her cousin added. "I brought you some kerosene."

Warren spent the day hauling wood for her fireplace and fixing up the chicken coop. He put a new wick in the kerosene heater that she used to keep the chicks warm, and fussed at her for ordering baby chicks during the winter months. "Your hens will start hatching their eggs come spring," he argued.

"Yes," she agreed, "and my chicks will be plump young fryers by spring."

Her cousin shook his head. "You work too hard for a woman, Mae Lee." He glanced out the window. "I see Hooker heading out to feed the mules. They're getting pretty old for farming, Mae Lee. Especially Maude. Hooker said she barely finishes eating her bundle of corn fodder at night."

"I know," Mae Lee said. "Old Molly's started to limp. Since Daddy left she hasn't been shoed right. Both mules are going down. First it was Starlight, and now the mules. I guess I'll just have to let go of the mules." She turned to face her cousin.

"There's talk that a lot of farmers are buying new tractors, Warren. I wonder what they'll do with their old ones?" Mae Lee asked.

"Either trade them in or sell them," Warren answered. "That's a mighty big step to take, Mae Lee. I know your daddy will understand if you don't farm the land for a year or two. They'll probably be back sooner than that anyway."

Mae Lee wasn't listening. "If I scrape up what I've saved back and take the money Mama's going to send for the children's new Easter clothes, I might can make a down payment on a used tractor."

Warren got up to add kerosene to the oil circulator. "You'd better hold on to that money, Mae Lee. With little children in the house it never pays to take out the last piece of money you have in your shoe. Besides," he added, "you never want to be forced to have to buy your seed and fertilizer for spring planting on time. Come fall, Mr. Kingsford can charge you whatever he wants to. Remember, with Hooker Jones working the land on the halves, you've got to put up all the money up front—to buy all the supplies."

Mae Lee pursed her lips. "Seems like the landowner puts up too much," she said softly.

Warren inserted a funnel into the heater tank and poured kerosene in. "The sharecropper carries a full load. He puts in all the labor and still pays half the expenses at harvest time."

"And gets half the profits," Mae Lee added quickly.

Since he had a few days off from his job, Warren promised Mae Lee he would ask Church Granger if he knew of a used tractor in good condition for sale. And to spare her from having to go to her parents while they were dealing with sickness, he would loan her what he could spare for a down payment on a tractor.

Later in the winter Mae Lee and Hooker set out together to check on a used tractor. It was a cold, windy Saturday. Hooker slowed his truck for the ruts in the dirt road. "Church Granger said this tractor is a good buy. I don't guess he would steer me wrong," Hooker said. "He never has before."

Mae Lee didn't know what she was looking for when she walked around the tractor. She merely duplicated every look Hooker Jones made. Somehow she felt she should. She nodded her head in agreement when Hooker Jones told the seller he thought the asking price seemed right much, but she didn't like it when he added that he'd be hard pinched to pay that much. It was her money, she thought, not his, that was being paid out. The least he could have done was say it would be hard for her. She said nothing, however; Hooker was old enough to be her father. Perhaps it was best that she'd remained quiet. The seller knocked one hundred and fifty dollars off the asking price.

In the cold truck with a nonworking heater, Hooker was gleeful. "We've got us a tractor and it's a fine one. Hardly broke in. I didn't let on how good it is."

Mae Lee pulled her scarf around her face. The cold air that blew in through the ill-fitting cardboard in the old pickup window chilled her to the bones. She was hungry. There would be nothing much for the Saturday supper, but she planned a really good dinner for Sunday. It seemed to her that if she could just scrape together a good Sunday meal, Saturday night didn't matter so much.

Before Mae Lee opened her front door, the smell of fried pork chops greeted her, but inside there wasn't a scrap of food in sight. The kitchen was clean and warm. She had only to read her children's faces to know they were hiding something from her.

Nellie Grace pulled her mother to a chair and put her hands over her eyes. "Don't look, Mama." Mae Lee didn't look, only listened to her children set the table and put out the food they'd hidden. When she opened her eyes she was truly shocked.

Her daughter Dallace had prepared her very first meal. She had cooked the food that Mae Lee had bought for Sunday dinner. She watched her son, Taylor, roll up his sleeves to his little elbows and wash his hands in a washpan on the wooden kitchen bench. "We didn't eat a bite of nothing all day long, Mama," he said excitedly. "We just all pitched in and helped cook." Mae Lee forced a weak smile and tried to appear happy. What the children didn't know was that they wouldn't be going over to their cousin Warren's house for dinner the next day. Not after what happened last Sunday, when Warren was away on duty and his wife Lou Esther had said what she said.

Last Sunday she'd done just like she'd done ever since her parents had gone—gathered up the children and headed for her cousin's house for Sunday dinner. Warren was what was called well-to-do. He wore his shoes shined, and a suit to work. He had taken Mae Lee and her children under his wing. Even when he wasn't in the area, the Sunday dinner was prepared for her family by his wife, Lou Esther. It was tradition.

Mae Lee had always felt welcomed and right at home for the weekly dinner, until last Sunday when her cousin was away working and Taylor, her fourth oldest, had asked for another helping of food, a single piece of chicken. There had been a platter still piled with fried chicken and more on the stove, even after everyone was ready for dessert.

Mae Lee had said no. "One piece is enough," she'd said.

"But I'm still hungry, Mama, bad hungry," Taylor said.

The hunger of a growing boy was in his eyes, so she gave him another piece. Lou Esther made no attempt to hide her displeasure. Her husband was away, and she was free to speak her mind. Her remarks were cutting and unkind: "Children who are fathered by worthless men are the hungriest children in the world."

Mae Lee didn't wait for her children to have the usual Sunday's two desserts, one of which was always a delicious nutmeg egg custard. Ignoring their pained, silent pleas not to have to miss dessert, she ushered them away from the table and straight out of the front door. As she marched her crying children home she made a sworn oath that she would never set her feet under Lou Esther's table for a meal for as long as she lived.

Now, the morning of the Sunday after the episode, Mae Lee stirred and sleepily opened her eyes. It was still half-dark outside. She reached out from under her warm layer of quilts and fingered the source of the cold wet thing pressed against her face. It was her littlest girl's nose. Her face and hair were dotted with melting snowflakes.

"It's snowing, Mama, snowing like crazy," Amberlee whispered excitedly. She slipped under the warm covers.

Mae Lee bolted upright. She had planned to be out of bed bright and early to gather a few turnips for dinner, before other farmers started passing her fields, going to church. Like her mama, so many of them felt it was a sin to harvest on the Sabbath. Now she would never find the turnips. It was probably just as well. Her children hated them anyway. She made a roaring fire in the fireplace and turned the oil circulator down. She needed to save oil. She scooped up the wild hickory nuts her son, Taylor, had hidden in the wood box and gave them to him to crack open and pick for brown sugar hickory-nut fritters.

By midafternoon, the children were hungry again. When the snow stopped, they begged to be allowed to go back to their cousin's house. They didn't say why; they didn't have to. Besides the food, there was a TV set at Warren's. Mae Lee felt regret over her rash vow. She shook her head sadly. Never cut off your tongue to spite your lips, she thought.

She was sifting the words of her vow through her mind again and again when Warren came to the door. He was not his usual self. "Well, what's the excuse?" Warren asked. "Dinner is almost on the table." He looked at the empty wood box. "I'll bring in more firewood from the porch while you get the children ready."

Mae Lee suddenly realized that her rash solemn vow not to

eat at Lou Esther's table again had not included her children. She had only spoken for herself. She had vowed, "As heaven is my witness, I will not set my foot under Lou Esther's table for Sunday dinner again"—nothing about her children. They were free to go.

She didn't have to lie to make an excuse for herself.

Dallace, her oldest, held her head high as her mama buttoned the top button on her coat. "Mama, tell Taylor not to eat up everything on the table this time. I hate it when Cousin Lou Esther's face turns into sour milk because he wants more chicken or something."

Mae Lee dropped her head in shame when she saw that Warren, standing in the doorway, had heard. She wished he hadn't.

"Oh, good Lord," he groaned, "so that was the fire that started the kettle to boil. I should have known Lou Esther said or did something. I still can't believe that my own cousin wouldn't at least tell me, though. Try to overlook Lou Esther, Mae Lee. You know how she is. She says things without thinking. She didn't mean no harm."

Taylor looked at his mama. "They better hold my hands then, Mama, 'cause I'm mighty hungry."

His mama pulled him close. "Eat all you can hold, son, and tote home all you can't." With a hug and the whisper "Eat, eat" to each one, she waved good-bye.

Afterward she scrounged for food in her kitchen. There had been more than enough for breakfast, even some leftovers. As always her son had been hungry, hungry, and had eaten every scrap of food in sight. Her mama had always said, "If there is a hungry child, a mother's hunger pain leaves." But Mae Lee's hunger pains were rising, increasing like the chill factor of winds that multiply the cold. She had a strong craving for fried chicken. It seemed that if it was Sunday, you should have fried chicken or fried something. They may not have had it during the weekdays, but nearly always for Sunday dinner. She thought briefly of her brood of young chickens in the small henhouse, feeding on cracked-corn mixture, warm in the dull glow of a smoky, slow-burning kerosene heater. All she had to fry was one of her biddies. The very thought of a fried biddy doused her taste for chicken. She glanced at the almost empty Coca-Cola jug in the kitchen corner. There was enough kerosene to last the night, but she'd have to head for the general store the next day. Monday was her day to deliver fresh eggs and shop for her week's groceries.

She made a batch of hot-water cornbread pancakes and loaded them down with homemade butter and sugarcane molasses. The homemade butter was from Mrs. Whitfield's house. After Starlight had died, she never owned another cow. She always got a week's supply of milk and butter in exchange for her children feeding and watering Mrs. Whitfield's cow. Her children wouldn't eat the butter at first; they claimed they saw her cat in the butter. Mae Lee told them cats didn't ever go near butter, but in the future Mae Lee made sure she was at Mrs. Whitfield's house from the time the butter-making started until she got her share. "I'll get the churn ready and churn the butter for you, Mrs. Whitfield," Mae Lee would offer, and would then use the wooden press to make a fancy mold.

"Why, Mr. Whitfield is going to be tickled pink when he

sees this on the dinner table," Mrs. Whitfield had said once. "Mae Lee, I know you always say you don't have time to cook for anybody but your family, but you don't suppose you'd have time to make up a fresh batch of those good buttermilk biscuits of yours? Daddy—" she paused and smiled, "that's what I call my husband sometimes—loves fresh buttermilk biscuits. But I can't seem to make good ones." Her eyes saddened. "I actually can't make any kind at all, Mae Lee. My mother didn't cook. And 'Cook' didn't want me fooling around in 'her' kitchen, as she called it, when I was growing up."

She sat nearby on a high stool while Mae Lee made the biscuits. She had a couple of dollar bills sticking out of the eyelet-trimmed pocket of her pink housedress. Mae Lee hoped they were for her. She was fresh out of sugar and coffee.

Mrs. Whitfield traced her fingers lightly across the smooth countertops. "My husband," she began softly, "would be glad to pay you whatever you'd charge if you'd agree to come in the late afternoon just to cook." When there was no immediate reply from Mae Lee, she hurriedly went on. "There would be no cleaning whatsoever. I just love to clean house."

Mae Lee glanced about and thought to herself, If you love to clean so much, why in the world don't you do it?

"Even Daddy says you work too hard on that farm," Mrs. Whitfield volunteered. "Farming the land is too hard for a woman—too hard."

At least you won't ever have to do it, Mae Lee thought. Mr. Whitfield was the county solicitor, but everyone knew that she was the one with the money. Ellen Whitfield didn't want for anything.

Mae Lee rolled out the biscuit dough. Her body rocked as though the rolling pin needed an extra push. "Farming is not too hard when it's your farm, your land, Miss Ellen. You see, that farm is mine, so it's not too hard at all."

She didn't offer Mae Lee the money in her pocket. Mae Lee had, after all, turned the cooking job down. Anyway, her butter was good, and she needed the milk for her children. In a small way, Mae Lee kind of thought that one reason why the Whitfields kept the cow was to make sure her children had milk.

Over a steaming hot cup of sassafras tea, Mae Lee envisioned what her children might be doing right now at her cousin's house. Maybe dinner wasn't ready when they got there. Perhaps they were sitting in the warm company room with the fancy doily-laden, deep wine velvet davenport, looking through Sears catalogs and watching TV. Lou Esther would most likely be in the same room, juicily licking her fingers to flip the catalog pages, sticking torn paper bag pieces between the pages to mark something she was sure to order. Mae Lee thought of the identical rose-colored butcher linen dresses they'd both ordered once. Looking through the wish-filled pages together, each had been careful to seem disinterested in the smoothly pleated skirt and rosy pearl buttons that fastened the simple top, lest the other decide, too, that it would be perfect for Sunday church. And that was exactly where they'd met, with their shocked faces greeting each other from opposite ends of the pew.

Her cousin's wife was probably getting up and down to make the few steps to the small kitchen to stir the trays of homemade ice cream freezing in her Kelvinator, and taking her time to put dinner on the table, not in the least concerned that Mae Lee's poor children would be starving. With fresh snow on the ground it would be quicker to make snow cream. Her children probably would have preferred it. Eventually the food would be ready, however, and with Warren home that Sunday there would be plenty for them.

The following spring Mae Lee realized how very right her cousin had been about the need to hold on to what money she had. She had to write and ask her mama for some money for seed, plants, and fertilizer. She didn't tell her mama that she'd had old Hooker Jones plow up every foot of clear farmland and plant produce. She knew all too well that her mama would once again urge her to try and find some good man to marry before she wore herself out working. Her mama would also fuss that Hooker Jones was too old for such a heavy work load. Once the farm work was caught up, she and Hooker planned to sell the corn, beans, okra, tomatoes, watermelons, and other field-fresh vegetables from his pickup in the back lot behind downtown Main Street.

Then near the end of summer, poor Hooker's wife Maycie fell sick again and was unable to help gather the crop. Half the time Hooker had to take care of her, and when the cotton-picking season started Mae Lee was forced to help. As soon as she got her children off to school, she made a daily morning trip to the little house where she used to live to take food to Maycie, before heading to the cotton fields to pick.

The warm sunshine from the mid-October sun streamed

down through the clear skies. It was midafternoon. Mae Lee stood and stretched her aching back. She took off her sweater and tied it around her waist. She glanced at her half-empty burlap cotton poke. If she stuffed the cotton into it well, she wouldn't have to empty it until she reached the end of the long cotton row. Next year, she thought, I'll ask Hooker to shorten the cotton rows.

Mae Lee worked alone, her hands moving from one cotton boll to the next as fast as they could go. At the rate she was picking, before the end of the week she'd have another bale of cotton ready to be ginned. The entire cotton crop would be finished before it was really cold, because once again it was a poor crop. It had rained almost every day during the late summer and early fall. The cotton was damaged and wouldn't bring a good price. Cotton was at its best if there was dry weather in the weeks prior to harvest. She remembered the years before DDT, when the boll weevil wiped out her daddy's cotton crop. Her daddy tried growing tobacco. The boll weevils didn't like it, but the young boys in Rising Ridge sure did. They stripped the leaves and smoked the green tobacco.

Even though the poor cotton yield meant little profit, Mae Lee didn't mind too much. She and Hooker had made good money with the summer produce crops, and with the profit from the cotton, though small, they would both come out all right. Best of all, Mae Lee would be finished picking cotton sooner. She hated to pick in the cold, and the fall days would soon be getting really cold. She hated it most when she had to brave the frosty mornings. The cotton work gloves, with the fingers cut off so her bare fingertips could grasp and pull the cotton from the bolls, were usually wet from dew or frost. They did little to keep her hands warm, and nothing at all to keep the hard, pointed, knife-sharp outer bark of the open bolls from puncturing and piercing her stiff, bleeding fingers.

From a distance Mae Lee watched her children walk up the narrow dirt road home from school. Taylor carried his baby sister's little primer. Little Amberlee was a year younger, but taller than her brother. Her older girls walked behind. She waved and called out to them. They didn't hear her. She was a little concerned that Taylor had not rushed to the cotton field where she was, the way he usually did, but instead had waited to see her at home.

Afterward, while she finished preparing the supper that Dallace had started for her, she watched Taylor slide into a chair. Mae Lee wanted to cook at least a part of the supper every night. Her daughter wasn't quite thirteen years old, too young to have to be the head cook in the house.

Mae Lee hugged her oldest daughter, "Smells good, Dallace. Now you go get your schoolbooks and study your lessons."

Taylor propped his elbows on the table and cupped his small face in his hands. He was small for an eight-year-old. "Mama," he blurted out, "where's my daddy? I wish my daddy would come back home, Mama."

At all times Mae Lee hated that question, but she hated it most at night. She poured cornbread batter into a large, black cast-iron skillet and slid it into the oven. She was in no hurry to answer her son's question. She closed the oven door, and looked directly at Taylor. "I don't know, baby, I really don't know." She lifted his little face upwards. "I'm going to go and feed the chickens, and when I come back inside I want to hear you helping your little sister read from her primer." Outside, Mae Lee fed her chickens and cried. When she went back inside Taylor was asleep in his chair.

At the supper table Taylor asked to be excused when he finished eating two wedges of hot buttered cornbread and a glass of buttermilk. He didn't eat any vegetables. Mae Lee thought he was too tired and sleepy to eat, so she made a little pallet for him on the floor near the new oil circulator, so he could rest until time for bed.

Mae Lee washed her children's socks and underwear and hung them on the backs of chairs to dry. She didn't want the dirty clothes to pile up. She was still feeling a little guilty about doing the washing the Sunday before. Her mama wouldn't have washed clothes on a Sunday no matter what. But it had been such a bright warm day. Mae Lee would have picked cotton that day if there had been no one to see her and think she had no respect for the Sabbath.

She had fallen asleep, and forgotten to move Taylor into his bed, when she heard him call out to her. "Mama, Mama, I hurt, I hurt, Mama." She rushed into the next room. Her son looked at her as if he was afraid. She felt his forehead. He was burning up with fever, and was talking crazy, out of his head, jabbering like a two-year-old.

She glanced at the clock. It was after twelve, the middle of the night. She covered her sleeping children, her little stair-steps she called them. She gently shook her oldest child. "Dallace, honey," she whispered, "Taylor is sick. I've got to get him to the doctor. I'm going to Church Granger's house. Take good care of your sisters and don't open the door for nobody but your mama."

She pulled on her pants and field boots, tied a belt around her cotton flannel gown and pulled it up under her heavy sweater and coat. She wrapped her sick child in blankets from his bed and hurried through the chilly October night to the Grangers'.

The bright moon cast eerie shadows from trees alongside the narrow path. She could feel the warmth of her son's feverish body. He was breathing harder. Her brisk steps quickened into a slow steady trot.

It seemed that, almost before she knocked, the front porch was flooded with lights and Church Granger was at the door. Maybe the dogs had barked. She didn't remember hearing them.

"My baby is sick," she cried. "I've got to get him to the doctor!"

Church turned quickly, walked to the foot of the stairs and called up to his wife. "It's Mae Lee, Liddie. Her son is sick. I'm taking her to Dr. Bell's."

"Wait," Liddie called back, appearing seconds later at the top of the stairs. Mae Lee watched her pull her robe about her as she hurried down the steps. She looked at the sleeping child in Mae Lee's arms. "Oh, Mae Lee," she moaned, "you had to carry him all the way here." She peered beyond Mae Lee. "Where are your children? I'll go get them and bring them here."

"No, no," Mae Lee hastily responded. "My Dallace won't

open the door. They'll be all right. She'll take care of her sisters."

Liddie turned to her husband. Her eyes were anxious. "Hurry, Church, hurry."

Church Granger tried to take the heavy child from Mae Lee's grasp, but her hold on her son was firm. The child felt almost weightless in her strong arms.

He drove faster than Mae Lee had ever ridden in her life. She held on to her son and pressed imaginary brakes to the floor every time he rounded a curve, but she didn't ask him to slow down. Instead she studied the moon that seemed to travel along with them, and tried to think about setting out to find her son's daddy. He had asked about his daddy. Taylor needed his daddy. She nestled her chin against his warm head. "I'll find your daddy," she whispered. The long country road seemed to stretch forward forever into the moonlit night, like the sometime worries of motherhood, long roads with no end.

As they drove on, Mae Lee thought about how concerned Liddie Granger had seemed over her little Taylor and her little girls at home. She remembered the day Liddie had been so worried over her own crying baby, she'd driven down to the cotton field where she and her mama were hoeing to ask for help. Mae Lee'd been furious seeing Liddie Granger drive her fine car down from her big fancy house on the hill. Now she couldn't believe that she had been so angry with Liddie for causing her mama to stop hoeing and go check on a crying baby.

* * *

At Dr. Bell's house, Church remembered he should have telephoned so he'd have been waiting for them. He called out to the doctor's barking dogs. "Be quiet, Duke, now, now, Trouble. Duke, Trouble, calm down, hush up."

"It's me, Bland," he called out, banging on the door, "Church Granger."

Dr. Bell took one look at the sick child. "Get me some cold water, Church," he said. "There is ice in the refrigerator." He put cold cloths on the boy's forehead and an ice bag at the back of his neck. He slid a thermometer under Taylor's tongue. When he pulled it out he shook his head. He didn't reveal the temperature. "Taylor's throat is really inflamed, Mae Lee. Nothing to be alarmed about, but I'll give him an injection of penicillin and keep an eye on him for a while." He took a small bottle from his medical bag and broke the snap seal. Tears rolled down Taylor's cheeks as the doctor injected his behind, but he didn't cry out. His mama obliged on that.

Church watched with Mae Lee as Dr. Bell changed the cold compresses once the heat from the child's body had warmed them. "Mae Lee," Church said, "I'm glad you came directly to me without waiting. I wish you had a phone so you could have just called us. With your parents gone, don't you struggle with those children alone. When you need help, call on me or Liddie."

"I did," she whispered, "and I will. Thank you."

After some time it was evident that Taylor was cooler and less restless. The ice packs had started to work even before the penicillin. As Dr. Bell took the child's temperature again, a relieved look crossed his face. He turned to Mae Lee. "The fever is going down," he said, then added, "but that doesn't mean it might not come up again. Be sure to keep him home a few days, and try to get him to take as much fluid as possible."

"I'll keep an eye on them," Church told Dr. Bell.

Once Taylor was well, he seemed to have forgotten about wanting to find his daddy. Mae Lee was grateful. The episode had finally confirmed in her mind what her divorce had put on paper, that she didn't want ever to lay eyes on Jeff Barnes again. Her child had been sick, and she had had to turn to a neighbor for help. If it hadn't been for Church Granger's willingness to oblige, Taylor might have died. She didn't know where Jeff Barnes was, but whatever the children might believe, he had spurned them, left his family to get by on their own without his help or caring or even, so far as she knew, curiosity. Biologically he might be their father but that was all. The children owed nothing to him but the fact of their birth, and she wasn't ever going to feel guilty again about them not having their father around, no matter what they might say. They would just have to get along without him.

: 6 :

Months before Mae Lee's daddy wrote that her mama had taken a turn for the worse, she had known that her mother was in poor health. In the summer of 1959, when her parents visited and stayed for some days while her daddy built a room onto the house for Taylor, she'd watched her mother's weak attempt to cook supper. "I'm so tired, Mae Lee, so tired," she whispered. She held the edge of the kitchen table and eased her body into a chair. "I think you'd better finish cooking supper, honey," she said.

Mae Lee had urged her mama to slow down. "You've been pushing yourself too hard. You've lost so much weight. Now that poor Grandma and Grandpa have passed on, you and Daddy need to move back so I can take care of you," she begged.

But her mama had insisted on staying down in Low Country. She said Sam had planted a few things and she'd stay on with him until after the harvest. She'd wrestled with her kidney ailment for quite some time, and would be all right, she said.

A short time later the news of her death came. Mae Lee left her children with Warren and Lou Esther and hurried down to Low Country to be with her daddy.

It was good that Warren brought the children down later. Despite her children's obvious discomfort and bewildered sadness, their presence at the ceremony helped their grand-daddy to handle his grief. It reminded him that there were still things to live for. Even so, when Warren urged him to return to Rising Ridge with them after the funeral, he was unwilling to go. Mae Lee didn't pressure her daddy to leave. He needed time alone, she reasoned, to unfold his grief.

She felt a part of the foundation of her life slipping away. Within the year, before her father could settle his wife's estate, he died suddenly from a heart attack. Mae Lee had recognized that when her mama died, her father seemed to lose his very will to live, yet knowing that still did nothing to prepare her for the blow. This time there was no point in bringing the children to the funeral. She left them with Lou Esther and went alone with Warren down to Low Country South Carolina to make arrangements for the funeral.

It was clear that her father had known his health was fail-ing. He had left a key in an envelope addressed to her, a key he knew she would recognize as the key to his strongbox. He had not written even a hint to its whereabouts. Apparently he trusted his daughter to know that, as in the old days, the strongbox would be securely positioned in some spot behind a board or plank with some special marking that would hold meaning only to an immediate member of his family. To find the strongbox Mae Lee had only to walk through the rooms of her grandparents' house and then point out a plank for Warren to take a crowbar to and pry loose. Inside the box, money was stuffed into small, brown paper bags and little cloth drawstring tobacco pouches. A rubber band held several insurance policies together.

In the several days that followed, Mae Lee went from room to room reluctantly placing household things and clothing into little piles. They were things she hated to leave behind, but, she told Warren, "I'm already wearing my mama's soul, I guess I don't need to add to the load." Later, just before they started to leave, she found the corncob doll her mama had made for her when she was a little girl. She wrapped the doll in an embroidered pillowcase and took it home with her.

Several weeks after the funeral, Mae Lee sat staring out of the window while her cousin Warren explained what he had done to settle their grandparents' estate in the Low Country. He'd made sure all the land taxes had been paid and didn't foresee any problem in selling the land. It was all good farmland. Warren advised her to hold on to the house and several acres around it. He'd overheard talk on the train when he was working as a porter that land in that coastal area was becoming increasingly valuable. "You'll be able to pay the taxes. Counting the money they and your mama and daddy had hidden away in the house, and the insurance policies, plus what the land will bring when it's sold, you're gonna be pretty well-off, pretty well-off, Miss Mae Lee," he said.

Warren pointed to the strongbox. "It's all locked in there.

It's a sad thing that the old people didn't know enough to put their money in the bank. We've come a long way, though. Little by little colored people are starting to catch up. I think you ought to get ready and let's go put it in the bank." He picked up the strongbox. "All of this money and not a dime of it in a bank, drawing interest. It's sad, really sad," he said.

Mae Lee turned to face him. "Maybe the reason I have the money they saved is that they *didn't* put it in a bank. Warren, don't tell me you've forgotten how poor folks down in Red Clay Valley lost every dime they had when the little bank there went under."

Warren shook his head. "But that was a long time ago. Banking is different today. They've got regulations, and the deposits are insured. Besides, what if the house had burned down?"

"It didn't, though," Mae Lee said, "but even if it had, it could have been just another way to lose it. If your money is gone, it's gone." She turned to face the window again.

"Mae Lee, Mae Lee." Warren stood up. "I'm gonna put everything under lock and key until you come to yourself, Mae Lee."

She didn't turn to face him. "Figure up what's owed you for all you're doing, Warren, and take something for yourself. You're kinfolk."

Warren shook his head. "I got my share a long time ago. They helped me buy my house and land. You worked to buy yours. With five children and no husband, you'll need everything you can get to put them through school."

Before he left, Warren made one last plea for Mae Lee to put that money in a bank. "You are right, Warren," Mae Lee conceded, "the money should be in the bank." She knew that very well, yet she listened to her heart. She decided she would put the insurance money and the money from the sale of the property in the bank, but she was going to keep the five thousand dollars that was in the strongbox hidden in her house. She would let Warren think she'd put everything in the bank; her daddy had once told her never to tell even her own children that there was money hidden in a house.

Mae Lee heaved a heavy, sad sigh. "Before you go back to work, Warren, if you get a chance, please take some of the money and buy a television set for my children. Maybe it'll take their minds off their granddaddy. They are too sad for young children."

: 7 :

In 1963, when the schools in Rising Ridge, South Carolina, were first integrated, Mae Lee accompanied her children to school every morning. It didn't matter that there had been no violence in the area. "Things can happen so fast," she told her younger children. "I feel better being here."

Mae Lee felt guilty about leaving her share of the farm work for Hooker and Maycie. It was, after all, fall harvesttime. But if there was no one to hire to take her place, the peanut crop would just have to be left in the fields. The peanuts would resprout and become worthless, but the farm would still be there. She wasn't quite so sure about her children.

Within the year, she stopped going along. It was the change in her daughters that stopped her. They were moving out of her world, and the name changes they made troubled her. Her daughters hated their names. Dallace quickly became Lacey, Annie Ruth was now Ann, Nellie Grace, Nell, and even her baby Amberlee wanted to be called just plain Lee. Well, they were probably right. It was a time for change.

During the sixties Mae Lee's concerns multiplied. The civil rights movement that had started to take shape earlier down in Alabama was gathering steam and momentum. That same year, when four black children were killed in the bombing of a Baptist church in Alabama, her son, Taylor, decided churches were no longer safe, so he refused to go. A few months later Taylor watched on television along with the rest of the nation as a little boy raised his hand in a salute to the casket of his father, the slain president. Taylor turned to his mama. "I don't know if my daddy is dead or alive," he said. "I'm going to leave to find him."

At age fourteen Taylor was so tall, so much like his father. For a fleeting moment it seemed to Mae Lee that it was Jeff Barnes who was sitting in the chair across from her. The tone in her son's voice cut her heart to the quick. Mae Lee felt the warm tears flood her eyelids. She held her breath, her eyes wide, didn't dare blink. When the hurting within her eased, she drew a long breath, pushed her chair away from the table, and left the kitchen.

She wanted to scream out at her son, at his father, wherever he was. But she didn't. She waited until the withheld sobs no longer shook her body and then she walked back into the kitchen.

Mae Lee put her hand on her son's shoulder. "I don't know when you are planning to leave, Taylor, but let me know in time so I'll have your clothes ready and something cooked for you to take with you." Her son burst into tears and left the room.

The next day after school, Taylor hastily pushed a little

brown paper bag in front of his mama and quickly left the room. Mae Lee opened the bag. Inside was a pretty white lace handkerchief. She smiled; the very first gift that she had received from Taylor when he was a little boy had also been a white lace–trimmed hankie. She thought of the warm early spring day when Taylor had presented it to her. She had been seated on the front porch with old man Joel Hanken. It had been a weekday, but Joel Hanken was all dressed up in his Sunday suit and necktie.

"You must have been to a funeral," she'd said, eyeing his attire.

"Nope, nobody dead that I know of."

"How come you so dressed up?"

"Well, sometimes there are other occasions that call for fixing up a bit."

Mae Lee watched his eyes, his sly grin. The sunlight on his scattered gold teeth made them glow like train lights in a dark tunnel. She could see the wheels turn in his mind. Joel Hanken was trying to be a sport. He had courting on his mind. That's exactly what he had on his mind, all right.

Oh, Lordy, Lordy, she thought to herself. I thought all the old widowers in Rising Ridge had given up on me. Despite her efforts to hide her loneliness, it must have shown. She was lonely, but she sure hated for everyone to know it. It was the spring weather, she decided, that had prompted Joel Hanken. Springtime seemed to be a troubling time for a wifeless man, especially if he was a farmer. She wasn't sure if the courting idea was for love, or only in hopes of finding a woman to cook and help with the upcoming crop planting and hoeing.

For the older ones, the coming of spring was just like putting high-test gas into an old car. It sure sparked them up.

Joel Hanken was still on the front porch, with Mae Lee shifting uncomfortably under his gaze, when her son, little Taylor, had raced into the yard from school. He glanced only briefly at his mama and rushed to the edge of the yard to spit. He drew a long breath of relief.

"I held it, Mama," he said. "I held it all the way from school. It was too awful to swallow, so I held it. I didn't spit around nobody, because you said a spitting boy and a crowing hen will always come to a bad end."

Mae Lee's little son had turned to meet his sisters. He made no effort to go inside to change his clothes as he usually did after school.

"Mind your manners," his mama coaxed gently. "We have a visitor."

The little boy eyed the visitor suspiciously, then climbed the steps and reluctantly offered his little hand. "We got work to do," he called out as his sisters approached, eager to prove that with him around, no other male was needed. Mae Lee watched her children tug and strain at an old tin washtub filled with rainwater. The tub wouldn't budge. She'd called out to them to stop before they strained their body muscles. "It's five of us, Mama," Taylor called back, "but it's only *one* of you."

Later that afternoon her son edged up to his mama holding something behind his back. In a small brown paper poke was the lace hankie.

"I bought it for you, Mama," he grinned. "Sold my own eggs to Mr. Baker. He said if a person ever saw a sad woman all they had to do was buy them something—and the sadness would go away, lickety-split."

"I'm surprised you didn't bring Fred Baker's thumb home. Every time he sells a pound of something he sells a part of his thumb. I'll bet he's sold that thumb a hundred times," she said. Then she laughed and hugged him.

Years later, Taylor told Mae Lee that when he saw Joel Hanken on the front porch that day, he'd wanted to send him away and find her somebody else who would be good enough for her.

Now Mae Lee tucked the new hankie her son gave her into the outside compartment of her pocketbook. Taylor would be certain to see it there and know it was her Sunday best. Taylor was special, always had been. She couldn't help wondering if her loneliness was showing again.

The civil rights revolution, spreading across the South, opened the way for Mae Lee Barnes's dream of educating her children beyond high school, in college. Even the small local colleges in South and North Carolina were opened up to blacks, and scholarships were made available to schools that before now had been just for whites. Yet her children chose, over the scholarships offered from across the country, to attend all-black colleges. Mae Lee felt deeply glad that they were proud of who they were, and secure enough to recognize that their educators had something of value to give as well. She also understood that her girls wanted to attend colleges where they could look forward to not just getting an education, but having some sort of social life as well.

Dallace was Mae Lee's only child to leave South Carolina to

go to college. Dallace went off to Fisk University in Nashville, Tennessee. Like all her sisters after her, she received a fine scholarship.

The English teacher at the high school encouraged some of the graduating girls to go to Fisk if they wanted to marry a doctor. "My daughter Dallace didn't marry a doctor, she became a doctor," Mae Lee would later brag, after Dallace earned a Ph.D. in psychology.

It seemed her daughters no sooner finished college than three of them set their sights on New York. Mae Lee's cousin Warren had been responsible for that. He had started telling them about the big money-paying jobs in New York that he'd heard about while working on the train. Mae Lee was uneasy about her girls leaving home, much less the South, to work up in the North. She wished Warren hadn't put the thought into their minds, and she told him so. "I don't like the idea of young girls working in big cities like that. They might end up staying and it's too far away from home," she said worriedly. "They've earned decent money working here in the South so far. Amberlee's always been able to always find a summer job, and after she finishes college this year, she'll find a steady job. They say there's lots of jobs in North Carolina. Now, you take Annie Ruth and the good job she's landed at A&T College in Greensboro, North Carolina."

In the end, her daughters won. Mae Lee knew Warren's widowed sister-in-law, Elsie Rae, who lived in New York, would take her girls under her wing. She could rest easy having them stay with her. Elsie Rae had been born and raised in a Christian home in Rising Ridge.

Having her daughters leave made it even harder for Mae Lee to handle her son, Taylor's, absence. It had been painful when her son was drafted for the Vietnam War, but somehow she knew he would have enlisted anyway. It was once again a troubling time for her.

But there was the farm to keep her busy. She spent long days working along with Hooker and Maycie in the fields, especially during the spring planting season.

It had been against Mae Lee's better judgment to plant so much cotton that year, but Hooker had argued that it was their most reliable cash crop. It was all well and good for him to say that. With the new two-row planter, all he had to do was drive the tractor and plant, plant. The trouble was, they had no mechanical weeder and cotton picker. They still had to handpick the cotton.

One day in late May 1971 there was an envelope in the mail without a return address written on it and with a Chicago postmark. She opened it, and unfolded a sheet of white paper on which was pasted a clipping from a newspaper:

JEFFERSON D. BARNES, 49, Elmhurst, May 4. Arrangements by Kilgore Funeral Home, Elmhurst.

That was all; there was no other information given, no signature on the paper. May 4 was three weeks ago. Perhaps it was one of her ex-husband's brothers who had sent it. Perhaps it was his wife; the chances were that he had married again. She had wondered sometimes whether Jeff had ever even known that he had been divorced; they had been unable to locate him to serve the papers on him, and the other members of his family had been long gone from Rising Ridge. Probably his wife—current wife? had there been more than one after her? who could say?—had come across her name somewhere in his belongings, and had been kind and decent enough to think that she might want to know. But if so, she obviously hadn't wanted to hear from her, or even for her to know who she was.

Curiously, she felt little emotion, and no grief. He had disappeared from her life and her consciousness so completely that it was as if she were reading about the death of a stranger or, at most, of a distant relative that she had hardly known. She would have to tell Taylor and the girls, of course. She would do that the next time they wrote or called. That was all there was to it.

At least there were the letters from her children—weekly notes from her daughters, regular batches from Taylor in Vietnam. She started opening the letters more carefully after she mistakenly tore into a ten dollar bill. Just something to add to your bank account, her children usually wrote about the enclosed money. Mae Lee was still a little afraid of putting all her money in the bank, though. So, just as she'd done with the money in the strongbox, she hid the children's money in her house. She didn't keep the money in the strongbox itself anymore, however; if anyone were to come in and start to look for money under the floorboards or something, that would be too obvious. Instead, she put the money in an old bag and kept it hidden around the house.

Aside from the money coming in from the children, the

farm was starting to turn a good profit. Mae Lee had started planting more and more summer vegetables. They were good cash crops. Hooker had built up a steady customer trade, including several small grocery stores that had standing weekly orders for the fresh produce in season. To get the orders ready for Hooker to deliver meant that Mae Lee, Hooker, and Maycie would have to start picking as soon as they had enough daylight to see. They were usually wet from the heavy dew before they were done, but the money they earned made it worthwhile.

Even so, Mae Lee had an uneasy feeling that bad was bound to happen before too long. Somehow, it just seemed to be the pattern of her life. When things were going really good for her, something would always pop up to take away her happiness.

The true reason for her concern was the fact that she hadn't heard from Taylor for several weeks. Then Taylor wrote to say that he had been wounded and was in the hospital in Hong Kong. In his letter Taylor didn't say how it happened. He simply wrote that the shrapnel in his right leg was mostly in the knee area and most of it wasn't too deep, and they thought they got it all.

Her daughters sought to comfort and assure her that Taylor was all right, and Taylor had written and said so himself. But Mae Lee couldn't seem to pull herself together. She was beside herself with worry.

In his next letter, however, Taylor was able to ease his mama's concerns. He wrote that he was really being well cared for. The nurses were wonderful, he said. They voluntarily went beyond the call of duty and spent their free time writing letters for some of the wounded and cheering them up. He told her about what they did and how much they helped.

One of the nurses even added a note at the end of Taylor's letter. "Dear Mrs. Barnes, Please don't worry about your son. He's getting along fine, and making a swift recovery. Rest assured that he is receiving every attention, and we're all looking after him."

Several weeks later Taylor wrote again, this time from a hospital in San Francisco. He would be there for the next four months, he said. Again he assured her that he was well taken care of. Thereafter, although Mae Lee wanted Taylor home as soon as possible, she worried less.

Mae Lee was glad that he was back in the United States again; she even thought of taking some money and going out to California to see him. Dallace and Annie Ruth, however, persuaded her to wait until Taylor was able to come home. "Mama, it's a long trip, and you'd just be in the way out there," Dallace insisted, "and you know Taylor would much rather for you to wait until he's all well again."

So Mae Lee waited for her son to come back to Rising Ridge that fall.

That summer found Mae Lee busy making plans for a wedding. Annie Ruth was engaged to Bradford Pierce, a young real estate developer from Greensboro, North Carolina. As excited as Mae Lee was about the wedding, she was even more so when she learned that her former classmate and longtime friend Ellabelle Ellis was moving from North Carolina back to Rising Ridge the week before the ceremony was scheduled.

Ellabelle wasn't moving back to the country, but would be living in town. It didn't matter to Mae Lee, as long as she was in the area. Ellabelle had an automobile, and could run out to see her anytime she liked.

Mae Lee scarcely gave Ellabelle a chance to unpack. "I'll help you do everything after the wedding," she promised. "Annie Ruth is marrying into a pretty high-class family. From what I hear, her in-laws are well-off. It's going to take a pile of money and a lot of work to get this place in shape for a wedding."

Ellabelle looked over the sunglasses resting on her nose. "Mae Lee, you've got to remember, the wedding is being held at the church, not at your house. The people coming here after the wedding will see only one thing, the food. We can get this place so prettied up, it'll make your fancy new in-laws wish they lived in the country."

Mae Lee leaned back in her chair. "I do have some money I can lay my hands on, but I can't put too much into one wedding. I've got four daughters." Mae Lee frowned as she looked across the nearby fields. "If I'm going to make anyone from town wish they lived here, I sure better help Hooker knock some of the witchweeds out of the fields, especially right near the house."

Ellabelle pushed her glasses up on her nose. "All I can see is pretty red and yellow flowers."

"Take your shades off, Ellabelle. I know it's been a long time since you lived in the country, but don't try to pretend you don't know that's witchweed blooming." Mae Lee laughed, but then grew serious. "I see Maycie heading somewhere with a hoe. It's mid-July, they ought to be caught up by now. Hooker is a good farmer, but he has a problem keeping the grass down. I really don't think he plows close enough." She stood up. "I can't stand seeing poor Maycie working in this heat alone. I've got to go help her."

"I thought you said Hooker Jones was working the land on the halves, Mae Lee," Ellabelle said.

"He is working on the halves," Mae Lee answered quietly.

"I bet you don't see white farmers out helping their share-croppers hoe," Ellabelle snapped.

"Maycie's ailing, Ellabelle," Mae Lee said sadly. She looked across the fields, her mind far from the wedding preparations. "You know, Ellabelle," she said, "after this year I'm never going to plant another cottonseed. I'm going to raise produce again. Hooker and I have turned a pretty good profit so far. As far as the rest of the land, I'll have Hooker plant soybeans. They say it's a good cash crop. At least we won't have to hoe and break our backs picking in the fall. You don't pick soybeans. I'll hire Church Granger to thresh them. He has a spanking brand-new combine. If I rent Warren's farmland that he never uses and plant that, along with what I have, I could come up with close to a hundred acres. Probably too much for Hooker to plant and plow. But I can always get one of Jonah Walker's sons to help out."

"Let me tell you, woman, you are something!" Ellabelle declared. "I wonder what Jeff Barnes would think if he was still alive and could see how you've turned this farm into real money. I'd like to see his face."

Mae Lee went inside. When she came out, she had on a

long-sleeved shirt, a thick layer of Vaseline on her face, and a straw hat in her hand. "Please say you'll be here early tomorrow morning to help me start getting things in shape for this wedding."

Ellabelle shook her head. "I'll be here, Mae Lee."

Mae Lee was starting to make a pot of coffee when Ellabelle opened the back door. "Rise and shine," she called out. "We've got a busy workweek ahead of us. Maybe we should have asked Lou Esther to come over and help us."

"She has her work cut out for her, so she'd better rest while she can; she's going to bake the cakes and pies."

By midmorning Ellabelle was hanging the curtains, starched and ironed, over the clean windows as soon as Mae Lee finished washing them. She backed away from a window, beaming over their work. "We make a pretty good work team," she proudly bragged.

"My girls won't know this place," Mae Lee said after they had rearranged all the furniture. "They'll be coming in just before the wedding and leaving right afterwards. They have to get back to their jobs in New York. Taylor's the one I'll miss seeing."

Taylor had written his mother from San Francisco that although he couldn't travel across the continent yet for the wedding, he was getting along much better and that he'd applied to and been accepted at Johnson C. Smith University in Charlotte for the fall term.

Mae Lee paged through a *Good Housekeeping* magazine with a tongue-dampened finger, thinking of the big fancy wedding the local minister's daughter had. There had been flowers everywhere. Mae Lee could just see her pretty daughter with a long train on her wedding dress trailing behind her as she walked down the aisle holding on to the arm of her cousin Warren. She closed her magazine and watched Ellabelle pull her mama's mismatched flowered cups and saucers from the cabinets to be washed.

"You know, Ellabelle, I clean forgot about flowers. I've got to find some. When Annie Ruth talked about having flowers sent in I told her that Rising Ridge had a florist. I couldn't see her sending in way overpriced flowers I'd end up paying for." She opened her magazine again. "On second thought," she said, "the more I think about it, it might not be a bad idea to just gather up wildflowers and ferns and bank the church with them. I think I remember seeing something like that on television once. There are blooming wild roses everywhere, and the ferns and moss alongside Catfish Creek are the prettiest I've ever seen." There was a faraway look in her eyes.

Ellabelle shook her head. "When I said to show your high-class future in-laws a side of country living, I didn't mean go to the opposite extreme. How could you get all the plants there and keep them fresh? You'll end up looking like you're too poor to paint and too proud to whitewash."

A satisfied look crossed Mae Lee's face. "Hooker Jones and I could do it. Everybody said we couldn't make a go of the farm but we did. We can pull this off too."

Ellabelle laughed. "Everybody also said, if you and Hooker weren't careful you'd forget and sell your front door steps and then wouldn't be able to get into the house."

Mae Lee showed Ellabelle a picture of a garden wedding in the magazine. "I think it'll be nice if we serve and eat outside in the garden after the wedding," she said.

Ellabelle stared at her friend in disbelief. "Have you lost your mind? I do believe the hot weather has dried up all the liquid in your brains, Mae Lee. It *would* be nice to eat in the garden, but you don't have a flower garden. And as far as eating outside goes, we'll have to, because we sure can't fit into this little place."

Ellabelle made Mae Lee a tomato-and-onion sandwich, smoothing on enough mayonnaise to choke a horse, and poured a glass of lemonade for her. She looked at her friend. "Mae Lee, if it weren't for your swollen ankles, you would look the same as you did your last year in high school." Ellabelle refilled her empty glass with lemonade. "If I'd had any inkling whatsoever that you were starting to marry off your daughters, I would have waited to move back to South Carolina until you were done. You should have asked the Lord to give you boy babies. Boys are easier." She laughed. "Boys are easier."

Mae Lee laughed, too. It was good that Ellabelle was back. She was a good friend. She had been the first one of her friends to marry and leave the farming community. Ellabelle's parents had always hated the sharecropping farming life. So, during the war, as soon as Ellabelle received the government insurance from her husband, her parents talked her into buying a house in North Carolina. Ellabelle always said her heart stayed in Rising Ridge, though. The air was different, she said; she missed the air of the piney woods.

Mae Lee had missed Ellabelle. She'd started getting along

better with her cousin Warren's wife, Lou Esther, in recent years, but they weren't companions. They didn't spend the better parts of the days talking. Still, Lou Esther was always there for her and the children.

On the day of the wedding she paid the children from nearly every family in the area to help Hooker Jones and his wife dig and cart in the ferns and moss from the moist banks of the creek. Lou Esther and Warren cut all the washed-out pink wild roses in the area, and didn't get a scratch on their hands and faces. They spread old pieces of canvas cloth and heavy burlap bags on the wood floors and banked the altar platform with the greenery and flowers. Elsie Rae, Lou Esther's sister down from New York, made and tied pink taffeta bows at just the right places. The old maid sisters, Honesty and Hattie Vee, who lived in the big, two-story house near the church, allowed every single red climbing rose they had to be cut and used in the church. So Mae Lee had her flower garden for the wedding after all. It was beautiful. She selected the Lord's Prayer and, at Ellabelle's request, Ave Maria to be sung at the ceremony. "They are perfect songs for a wedding," she said. They set the stage for themselves as well as for Annie Ruth; the songs were just the right touch to make two old friends cry.

Standing and watching her daughter repeat sacred vows, Mae Lee felt the pain of her parents' death. The joys of seeing her children going to college and getting married were halved by the absence of her parents.

No one noticed that there was no flower garden for the reception at Mae Lee's house. The surrounding trees made a bower of shade, and the neighbors' cut flowers made the yard appear to bloom.

The day after the wedding, Mae Lee and Ellabelle sat under the shade trees. Mae Lee soaked her feet in a small tub of warm water and Epsom salts. She looked in the direction of the Granger house. "Now that's a mansion if ever there was one," she said, adding, "you probably won't believe this, Ellabelle, but back in May, as soon as their baby boy graduated from high school, Liddie Granger packed up and left Church Granger."

"I don't believe it!"

"I knew you wouldn't."

"You mean to tell me Liddie Granger left that fine house?" Ellabelle questioned.

"It's not the house I think about a woman leaving," grunted Mae Lee. "It's Church Granger I think about. Everybody talked about what a wonderful father Church was, how he took his boys hunting and fishing and bought each one a new car the day they got a driver's license." Ellabelle moved her chair so she would have a better view of the Granger's house.

"Not too many women can walk away like Liddie Granger did. It's going to be hard for the boys coming home and there's no mama in the house. She just up and left." Mae Lee drew a long breath. "Liddie Granger will probably regret what she's done."

Mae Lee never forgot the kindness Church Granger had shown her the night Taylor was so sick. During the months and years that followed, he had helped her with various things. She didn't care what anybody said, Church was not only rich-rich, but was a kindhearted and caring man. Yet his wife hadn't found him so wonderful, or she wouldn't have taken up and departed so abruptly.

The day Taylor came home from the war, Mae Lee and Ellabelle waited at the tiny Greyhound bus depot in town for almost an hour in advance of the scheduled arrival time. Mae Lee had worried that the bus might come in early, or that Ellabelle would have a flat tire on her car on the way in. It was a fair day with a cloudless sky, yet she also worried that it might rain and the small wooden bridge they had to cross would be flooded over. She'd gotten out of bed in the wee morning hours and started cooking, so they could get an early start.

Although the women well knew the direction the bus would come from, as they stood waiting they constantly turned their heads, like a pendulum on a grandfather clock. When the bus finally arrived and braked to a swooshing stop, Mae Lee and Ellabelle stood on tiptoes to try and catch sight of Taylor. At first it looked like he wasn't on the bus. But when Taylor finally came down the step, all dressed in uniform, he looked so much like his daddy, Mae Lee couldn't believe it wasn't Jeff come back to life.

It seemed Mae Lee had waited forever for her son to come back. To have him home for such a short time! Before she had time to listen to all his war experiences, her only son was married, then off to college, and then teaching school.

When Taylor graduated from college and received his diploma, Mae Lee stood and applauded. He's a fine young man, and he's going to be a good teacher and father, she thought as she settled back into her seat.

Part : III

: 8 :

In the months and years that followed Annie Ruth's wedding and Taylor's return from the war, Mae Lee all but stopped working in the fields. If she wasn't planning weddings or helping with newborn grandchildren, she was being called upon for some other thing. It seemed that Annie Ruth's marriage opened up the floodgate for weddings. Dallace was the next. Her wedding set the stage for Nellie Grace. As soon as she got back to New York from attending Dallace's wedding, Nell called home. "I'm in love, Mama, and I want to get married. Please say it's all right," she said. Mae Lee gave her permission and she was married the next day. It all reminded Mae Lee of the time she'd asked her mama's permission to get married. Nellie Grace was a computer specialist, and off on her own, yet she'd asked, though what she might have done if Mae Lee had objected was another matter. In a way, it was all kind of nice for Mae Lee. She enjoyed the fuss her new sons-in-law made over her.

Finally there came a year when Mae Lee and Ellabelle had nothing to make plans and get ready for. And though they openly expressed their relief, inwardly they felt a little deprived. And then, as always, there was the bitter surfacing along with the sweet. The happiness over one event was dampened by the sadness of another. Mae Lee hadn't been spared. After a very short marriage, Nellie Grace was getting a divorce.

Lost in thought, Mae Lee leaned back in her rocking chair. Ellabelle sat quietly nearby; her grown children had always lived away from Rising Ridge. The two widows had come a long way. Both lives had often been a long hard row to hoe. Mae Lee's children were all grown and away. Dallace and Nellie Grace were still in New York, Amberlee just across some river in New Jersey. Mae Lee didn't think she'd have to worry about a wedding for Amberlee anytime soon. They all had good jobs, Mae Lee thought, and for the time being, two of them had good husbands. Annie Ruth, bless her heart, quit her job to stay home with her children. Taylor had decided to accept a teaching job in his wife's hometown, Overrun, just outside Concord, North Carolina, a little more than an hour away. With Annie Ruth in Greensboro, North Carolina, at least she had two children reasonably close by.

The women were quiet for a long time. Finally, Ellabelle spoke. "For right now my children are all doing well, really well. I think we should be very content and happy, but I'm not. Wonder why?"

Mae Lee swallowed hard. "Maybe, because like me, you're

lonely." Mae Lee quickly brightened, though. "I won't be lonely long," she said. "My little grandson Tread is coming this summer." Her thoughts shifted to the farming season just ahead, and she asked her friend if she'd be available to carry her a few places to take care of some business the first of the week.

On Monday morning, Mae Lee woke early and called Ellabelle on the telephone. "You didn't forget me, did you? I know it's early but you know how long it takes to get waited on down at the Farmers Center this time of year."

"I'm still in my bed, but I guess I'll be there by the time you're ready," Ellabelle said.

Later that morning she stopped Hooker Jones from his plowing to tell him that the fertilizer and soybeans were ready for him to pick up from the Farmers Service Center. "It's all paid for," she said.

Mae Lee's days were filled with happiness during the summer her grandson spent with her.

"I want to be a doctor, grandmama, a medical doctor," he announced one day, clear out of the blue. She was getting ready to shell peas and he was playing in the sand.

It had pleased her, so she put off her peas, summoned Ellabelle, and they drove into town in search of a toy medical bag. As they drove along in the late afternoon, the outline of the sun's rays streamed down through the clouds, fanning out like an oversized pleated lampshade. "The sun's rays are drawing up water from the earth, collecting moisture," Mae Lee pointed out to her grandson. "It's going to rain in a few days."

The little boy let go of her hand and gazed out the window at the sun. The clouds that had seemingly anchored around the edges of the sun had slowly worked loose and were drifting away.

"Don't look too long at the sun, Tread. Not even when it's cloudy. It'll cause you to go blind." She told him the things her mama had told her.

Her grandson reached for her hand again.

"Ouch," she screamed out in mock pain. "That finger is going to need a Band-Aid, doctor."

He loved her world. She loved his.

After they had gone looking in every store on Main Street, they returned empty-handed to the car where Ellabelle was waiting. Mae Lee glanced at her watch. "We've got to hurry and find that bag. The stores will be closed before we know it. That little variety store that opened up across town might have a little doctor's kit, but I don't know if we can make it before they close," Mae Lee fussed. "With your slow driving, Ellabelle, we walk wherever we go, even when we are riding in your car."

Ellabelle handed her the car keys. "Why don't you drive, since you think you can wheel it so fast?"

All they were able to find was a little plastic nurse's kit. Mae Lee bought it anyway. She cut a picture of a little boy from a catalog and pasted it over the little girl's face on the kit. If only they had gotten an earlier start that day, they could have driven to North Carolina where they had the big stores and would have found her grandson a male doctor's kit.

In time her little Tread's medical practice went a little too far. One day she found him instructing his playmates to take off their clothes. So she took his nursing kit away.

: 9 :

Mae Lee looked across the fields of smooth ground. During the winter she had worked with Hooker and Warren to clear and burn off the strips of brush and undergrowth that crisscrossed her farmland. Now the seventy-some acres, including the portion leased from Warren, stretched out before her. She inhaled the clean smell of freshly plowed soil and listened to the din of tractors plowing or disk-harrowing throughout the countryside. Warren and Hooker had been right that she should buy a tractor. It could do more work in an hour than a mule could in half a day.

Mae Lee liked the way the land spread out before her. If her cousin Warren ever decided to sell, she sure wanted his land. She thought of asking him about it, then changed her mind. Warren had retired and might want to sell, but she didn't want to put the idea in his head. What money she had hidden away was doubtless enough to cover his asking price.

She turned to look at the land near the house where her children were born, where Hooker and his wife lived now. That was the farmland where the sweet potatoes should be grown for the current farm season. She would be sure to remind Hooker of that—once he had planted the ground crop in the same spot as the year before and all the sweet potatoes developed rotten spots.

Farmers need to stay close to their land, not only because they love it, but because they have to be there. She thought of how she'd almost lost her entire crowder pea crop to worms the summer before. She'd been called to New York to take care of her little sick granddaughter, Shella, while her daughter Dallace was away for some work conference. Poor old Hooker had been anxious to get ahead with his planting and had planted the crowder peas before June. And unless one uses a powerful amount of pesticide sprays, worms will eat up peas planted so early in the season.

Mae Lee slowly made her way back up to her house. The old dirt road was paved now. There was a stack of letters in her mailbox, one from each of her children. She knew before opening them that they were to remind her about the trip to Greensboro, North Carolina. The letters were brief.

Mother,

If you need anything before Annie Ruth's kid's graduation, let me know. I'll call you on Sunday. Hugs and kisses from Tread and Shella. See you in North Carolina.

Love, love,
Dallace

Dear Mama,

Can't wait to see you at Travenia's graduation. Don't buy a dress, I am bringing you one. I think it's just right for you. I luv you, Mama.

Nell,
oops . . . Nellie Grace

Dearest Mama,

Great news! There is talk that I just might be named head librarian here! Of course, it's only a small branch, but it's a step in the right direction. I told you that a master's degree in Library Science would pay off.

Love you,
Amberlee

Dear Mama,

Can you believe the great graduation day is almost here? I'll pick you up at nine in the morning on the Monday before, and we'll be off to Greensboro.

Bye Mama,
Your son Taylor

P.S. I may be a little late.

The last envelope was the fancy graduation invitation from Annie Ruth. Inside was a note and two crisp twenty-dollar bills.

In case you have to go to the beauty shop or need a little something. We await your visit.

Your daughter,
Annie Ruth

The day they were to leave for Greensboro, Taylor arrived at his mama's house an hour early. Mae Lee was still in her robe. "I'm hungry, Mama," he announced.

"I know," she said. "I fixed your plate and put it in the oven. I thought you said you were going to be late."

"I was up early so I just left."

After Taylor finished his breakfast, he pushed his plate back, dropped his head into his folded arms resting on the table, and went to sleep. Mae Lee woke him up when they were ready to leave. "The baby kept us up most of the night," Taylor explained. "She's teething again. I really hated to leave Bettina with the baby so fretful."

Mae Lee patted Taylor on the back. "You are a good husband, but you can rest easy with your mother-in-law there. She knows how to care for babies." Later, having thought more about the baby, Mae Lee told Taylor, "I really feel I should have kept my grandbaby and let Bettina make this trip."

"Bettina wouldn't have come, Mama. She's a homebody. I have to beg her to visit you, and even then she always finds some excuse, and you know how much she cares for you." Taylor sounded unhappy.

"Well, if you want to know how I personally feel about this trip, son, I think it's a waste of time. All this fuss over some little old grade school graduation. You'd think the child was graduating from college. It's a waste of money," she fussed. "And I'm going to tell Annie Ruth so, 'deed I am."

Taylor reached to turn his radio down. "I wouldn't say nothing, Mama, you know how Annie Ruth is. She likes to do things in a big way."

After they arrived at Annie Ruth's house it wasn't so easy for Mae Lee not to say anything. "My son's daughter is the first black child in this town to graduate from Knowlton Hills Academy," Lottie Pierce, Annie Ruth's mother-in-law, bragged.

"And she just happens to be my daughter's child as well," Mae Lee added.

Mae Lee watched Lottie Pierce walk away, her arms held straight out from her body like the arms of a homemade corn-cob doll, stiffly held in place by bulging pillows of fat. She looked down at her own thickened body. "If I weren't con-stantly cooking for my children's parties, I wouldn't be in this shape," she complained to Annie Ruth.

She spooned damson plum custard into fancy pastry shells. "Let me tell you something, Annie Ruth, you better gag my mouth when your mama-in-law comes back to pick up the desserts. If she starts up with this debutante talk, and how a real lady never changes to a different perfume from one day to the next—and how she only wears one fragrance, and how she, unlike a lot of 'us,' saw to it that her other granddaugh-ter wore braces, I am going to have to ask her while she was doing all that, why didn't she have them work on that child's bowlegs when she was a baby? They had braces for them, too. Right off I made sure my Dallace had them for her son Tread so he wouldn't be bowlegged and pigeon-toed."

After her daughters finished fussing with her hair, Mae Lee looked in the mirror. Much as she hated to have to say it, she could remember only a couple of times when she'd looked so good. From the moment she laid eyes on the dress Nellie Grace bought for her, she'd loved it. That soft mauve had always been a good color for her complexion.

Long before the graduation exercises were under way, Mae Lee's thoughts of the waste of money had vanished into thin air. She was unquestionably the proudest person there. "My granddaughter is the third from the left on the second row," she pointed out to the woman seated next to her.

Afterward, at the reception, she hurriedly pulled out pictures to show anyone she met.

Amberlee looked at Nellie Grace. "Promise me if I ever have children and start from day one trying to put them on the phone to talk, and start showing their pictures to every stranger I meet, promise you will cart me off to see a shrink as fast as you can."

Nellie Grace grinned, "On my Girl Scout's honor I promise, even if I've never been one." The childless sisters shared a private giggle.

: 10 :

During the early 1980s, the exodus of the blacks from the rural farming area to the North after World War II ended was reversed by their return. Mae Lee Barnes watched and listened to much-changed speaking voices shifting in and out of varied accents when they told questionable stories about their very successful northern jobs and businesses.

Within a few years a small black section near the edge of town was dotted with the new construction of modest, two-bedroom brick homes with wall-to-wall carpet and carports or two-car garages—houses that for the new owners defied any description short of a mansion, although to Mae Lee's way of thinking they were awfully tiny and crowded together. Still, Mae Lee had to confess to herself that she was a little jealous, especially after Ellabelle made the decision to buy a house in the subdivision.

When Annie Ruth and Dallace visited in 1985 along with their husbands and children, they sensed how lonely Mae Lee was out there in the country by herself, especially since Warren and Lou Esther had started staying on and off in town with Lou Esther's aged sick aunt, while Hooker Jones's wife Maycie was in and out of the hospital most of the time.

When her daughters were ready to leave Mae Lee seemed so uneasy and lonely that they stayed on for another day. Earlier that year, Taylor had mentioned to his sisters how lonely it was for their mama living all alone in the rural countryside, and suggested that they encourage her to move to town. But she'd always seemed so cheerful when her daughters called or visited, they believed Taylor had misread her feelings. Still, when one of her sons-in-law spoke about a move to town, Mae Lee surprised everyone by agreeing that it might be worthwhile to buy a small house in town, closer to where Ellabelle lived.

Mae Lee's Realtor son-in-law Bradford shook his head. "Mrs. Barnes, you don't want to buy a house in the section of town I believe you're thinking of." He turned to his wife Annie Ruth for verification. She nodded her head, yes. Bradford continued, "I can see you building a house at the end of that section, Mrs. Barnes, but not buying and living in one of those little boxes in it. They're too cramped, and they won't hold their value for very long."

Taylor had said the same thing when she hinted she might buy like Ellabelle did. In Ellabelle's whole neighborhood there was in fact no house, new or old, nice enough for her to leave the country to live in. But just at the edge of the section, where the street widened and became a road, there were several large lots where a house could be built that wasn't so small and boxy and jammed up next to its neighbors. It was inside the city limits, yet there was land, and trees, and room to plant a garden, and maybe even a few fruit trees. It could be a nice house, with several spare bedrooms for when the girls and their families visited.

To all the people she grew up with who had moved away, Mae Lee wanted to prove that it hadn't been a bad idea to stay in Rising Ridge. Maybe continuing to live down in what some called the boondocks hadn't been the fashionable thing to do back in the 1950s and 1960s, but now, when her old friends and classmates would come back to Rising Ridge with all their city airs, looking upon her as down-at-the-heels country, she'd have something for them to see. She'd show them.

Mae Lee was surprised that her children moved so quickly in getting the land and the new house under construction. A bank loan was easily granted, but she hesitated signing off on her land until Warren and Taylor assured her she wouldn't be liable for too much, because her children had put down a sizable down payment. She had not known at the time that a big chunk of it came from Nellie Grace's divorce settlement. That, coupled with the children chipping in on the monthly bank payments and a son-in-law who was a builder, made it possible.

Mae Lee asked Bradford, her son-in-law, to please put a lightning rod on the roof of her new house, and while they were up there to kindly put up the rooster weather vane she'd saved for years.

* * *

On moving day, in the summer of 1986, Mae Lee's children and grandchildren were on hand to help her make her move from the farm to the new house in town.

Mae Lee's daughter Dallace had forewarned her not to be overly concerned when she saw her grandson Tread. "Tread has had an earring put in his ear," she said. "But the earring doesn't imply what you think. It's in the left ear," she'd explained.

Mae Lee had been so angry. "What *am* I thinking?" she questioned. "What am I supposed to think? So, it's in the left ear. Left ear, right ear. It doesn't amount to a hill of beans what ear it's in, Dallace. He's wearing an earring, isn't he? What difference does it make where he wears it? I'm like the Ninevites in Jonah's day. I don't know my right hand from my left. What am I supposed to think, is he or isn't he?"

"Don't be silly, Mama," Dallace had said. "You don't know anything about kids nowadays."

The first time Mae Lee saw the earring in her grandson's ear she had pretended not to notice. Anyhow, Tread worked pretty hard to keep the earring out of his grandmother's sight. One evening at the dinner table, he leaned near her. "Grandmama," he'd said softly so everyone wouldn't hear, "I don't think I'll care for a helping of summer squash, thank you." And, as always, she'd put a spoonful or two on his plate, and like always he'd made a teasing face and had eaten them. He was the same old Tread, earring or not.

The next day, after they had all gone home, she felt at loose ends. From dawn until time for bed the house was quiet. Mae

111

Lee was lonely. There were too many empty beds. Too much, too late, she thought. Reminders of her children were scattered throughout the rooms, Amberlee's doll, Taylor's baseball cap, the things her grandchildren left behind. She wished her children were still there, still little and underfoot.

She gazed half-interestedly at the television, half-listened sometimes to medical advice that nearly always left her with what she thought was a new ailment in her body. I'll have to talk with my doctor Dallace about that, Mae Lee thought to herself. It didn't matter to her that, as Dallace more than once had reminded her, she was not a medical doctor.

Mae Lee never came out and said it, but she didn't really care too much for the overrated silver years of retirement. Yes, she was proud of her children, pleased that they had been well educated and held down good jobs. But there was an emptiness in her life. She wondered sometimes what it might have been like if Jeff Barnes hadn't left her, what kind of life they might have had together. She had no doubt whatsoever that he would have loved his children and would have been pleased over how well they had turned out.

Still, the decision to move to town had been a good one. So many of her old friends lived nearby now. The chairs on her front porch never remained empty for long. As soon as it was shaded from the summer's hot sun, Mae Lee would leave the air-conditioned comfort of her living room and sit out there, her very presence an open invitation to the neighbors, her porch a welcome mat. Through idle conversation spiced with gossip they reviewed the events of the day, and the years that brushed their lives, exposing and hiding faults as if they were removing layers of paint from old furniture or doing a touch-up job on the town.

"Poor Clairene's troubled again, Mae Lee," Ellabelle announced sadly one day even before she climbed the steps.

"How come you say that Clairene's troubled?" Mae Lee asked. She didn't look up, just kept on shelling peas.

"Can't you hear her? She's singing 'Amazing Grace' again." Ellabelle climbed the steps. "Get me a bowl, and I'll help you shell peas." She pulled a handful from a big brown paper bag. "You must be having the preacher for supper tonight."

"No, just me."

"It's enough for three families."

"I'll put what's left over in the freezer."

Ellabelle lifted her skirt to wedge a pot between her fat thighs.

"For goodness' sake, woman," Mae Lee fussed, "pull your dress down! You might excite somebody. As if it were possible," she added.

Ellabelle grunted, "Huh, it's possible all right, and that's exactly what I want to do, or run 'em crazy, one. Just might snare me an old nighthawk. He'll be good for the night and can fly off in the morning. This old tired body could stand a little tune-up. My engine parts have been neglected too long."

"Hush up," Mae Lee laughed. "You are going to mess around and start talking dirty. With the state of mind you're in, it wouldn't be safe for old man Sheets Cannon to walk by."

Ellabelle grunted. "I know you don't mean Sheets. My body engine parts are not that much in need of repair. Poor Cannon was born troubled. His mama had to be also, to have a last name like Mills and then turn around and name her son Cannon. How could he escape being called Sheets? Especially the way he keeps his head tore up. Poor thing, he's always three sheets in the wind."

Mae Lee laughed. "I guess it's better than being called Pillow Case or Towels. They say he was fired last week from the textile mill where he was working."

"I thought he retired when he was sixty-five."

"He did, Ellabelle. He was just doing odd jobs part-time. They say when he got his walking papers he asked to speak to the head man to thank him for being able to work there for so many years. Well sir, they said, Sheets took off his cap and sort of bowed, 'I want to thank you, sir, want to thank your kinfolk, but most of all I want to thank your mother for doing something nobody else has *ever* done, and that's birth a SOB like you!' Then the tipsy fool started singing, 'What you gonna do, when the river go dry . . . sit on the bank and watch the catfish die . . .' and then he truck-danced out of the office."

Ellabelle laughed until she cried, then she took off her glasses and lifted the edge of her wide skirt to wipe the tears from her eyes.

"There you go again," said Mae Lee. They laughed some more. She grew serious. "At least while he lives with his sister he won't go hungry for something good to eat. Sheets's sister is a good cook. Cooked for years for some of the richest people in Rising Ridge."

"*Was* a good cook," Ellabelle corrected. "She's getting old now. Last year she forgot to remove the plastic bag from the inside of her Thanksgiving turkey. Poor thing. She just wasn't

114

at herself that day. She's a good woman." She glanced at the early summer's sky. "Before you know it we will be hearing the honking Canadian geese streaking across the skies. My daddy said it was going to be a cold, cold winter if they formed letters when flying. For me they spell 'almost turkey time.'"

Mae Lee reached for more peas. "How can you think that far ahead? It's after mid-October when they fly through."

"These peas are making me hungry, that's how."

After they'd cooked and eaten a Sunday dinner on a weekday they returned to the front porch.

Mae Lee took a long sip of iced tea. "I swear this is my last glass." She swallowed hard. "We got to stop eating so much. We're pushing our bodies way out of shape. Did you see Janet Dalton's fancy picture in the paper today? She sure looked good."

"I would too," Ellabelle pined, "if I had her money. She probably uses what my daughter said most of Them use nowadays, something I think she said called Night Repair. She works at the cosmetic counter in Dillard's department store, you know. According to my daughter, a little bottle no bigger than my thumb is very expensive!"

"If it's the size of your thumb, honey, it's a pretty good-sized bottle," Mae Lee chuckled.

"Look who's talking, child, you must still be looking at your body in your high school mirror."

Mae Lee laughed. "It's pitiful the way we've let ourselves go. Maybe we need some of that night cream."

"A lot of us widows need it, especially poor old Miss Austin who runs the jewelry store on Main Street. For all I know she might be using it. If the stuff does work, its repair job sure doesn't last, because by daybreak it's broken down and needs to be fixed all over again." Ellabelle shook her head.

"I almost hate to go in her store anymore," Mae Lee said. "She is so anxious to find a friend, before she even waits on her customers she'll ask, 'Do you know of any good unmarried men around?' I guess she's teasing, though."

Ellabelle poured iced tea from a pitcher. "Like hell she is. I was in there to get a battery for my watch and with my own ears I heard her tell a customer that she'd heard that old Clay Lewis had started taking some high-powered pep pills, so she said, 'I called up Mr. Clay Lewis one evening, and I said to him on the telephone, come on over. I'm a-sitting here all alone with nothing on but my TV.'"

"Poor thing, she's still searching for love. The likelihood of finding it, though, is about as good as a dry dandelion flower staying on its stem during a windstorm," Mae Lee said sadly.

Clairene's singing was slicing through the still night air again, her voice clear and mournful: ". . . I once was lost, but now I'm found . . ."

They listened, and from a distance quietly shared her sadness.

Ellabelle wiped away tears. "Lord, Lord, Clairene can sing."

She'd hardly finished speaking when Clairene's husband, Joshua, slowly drove by, his arm in the open car window. From a radio turned up too loud for a man his age, a mellow voice offered the blues. She watched him snapping his fingers to the beat.

Mae Lee shook her head sadly. "Poor Clairene, I'll bet her

116

old man has gone and overbit too big a chew of tobacco again. She's going to have to sing more than 'Amazing Grace' to hang on to that big new white Lincoln he's tooling around in all over town."

"I don't know how I even have time to fill my head with someone else's problems," Ellabelle said, "I'm up against so much. My children are putting me through right much now. You got good children, Mae Lee." Ellabelle seemed really sad. "Guess it does no good to talk about it, though."

"Children always seem to offer some problems," Mae Lee mused. "I heard my Taylor's spoiled wife Bettina threatened to pack up and go back to her mother's." Mae Lee drew a deep breath. "I am careful not to interfere with my daughter-in-law and my grandchildren. The only problem, to tell the truth, that I'd have with Bettina leaving is that she'd soon be running right back to my son. Taylor is not only a fine schoolteacher, he's a fine husband!"

Mae Lee softly fingered the pin on her dress. A découpage photo of a grinning little boy, her grandson, Dallace's child, lay enshrined in a pseudoantique cameo pin wreathed in tiny plastic pearls. A printed nametag was never necessary for Mae Lee. The picture of her grandson was her identity, her reason for being. Mae Lee was the grandmother of Tread Wallace.

Mae Lee offered no apology for singling out her grandson for extra praise. He was the firstborn male of her grandchildren, not to mention being very special besides. She thought of the times when, as a youngster, he would beg and cry to come stay with her, beg and cry to not have to leave. She loved his little sister Shella, too, but disapproved of the way she was being raised. She was a spoiled brat. "She is a precocious little girl," her daughter Dallace had tried to explain. Her daughter may have had a lot of learning to be able to become Dr. Wallace, Mae Lee thought, but she sure raised a rotten kid in the process.

Unlike Ellabelle, Mae Lee had not used her tears for Clairene's singing. She needed them now. "My grandson," she moaned softly, cupping her hand over his picture, "my fine baby boy. He's got an earring in his ear. An earring. And you know something, his mama is to blame. Yes, my daughter Dallace is at fault."

"For heaven's sake, Mae Lee, the boy is almost fourteen years old. You know how these teenagers go out for these stylish fads," said Ellabelle.

"Style? You know deep down in your heart what people think."

"People don't think nothing if it's in their left ear."

"All I know is for the first and only time in my entire life, I'm not sorry that my mama is dead. I never believed I would or could ever say this, but I know if my mama wasn't dead, this would kill her. Would kill her for sure."

"Mae Lee, I'm gonna tell you like they do on TV—'You can see what it's doing to someone else, but you can't see what it's doing to you.' Let it go. Listen to me, somebody who knows."

Mae Lee looked at her friend. She believed Ellabelle remembered everything she'd seen and heard on TV. But she couldn't always put too much stock in some things she had to say. How could she? There is not much there for a woman who answers when asked if she has a middle initial, "I don't know

118

whether I have one or not. I have a middle name, though. Maybe you could use it instead." It seemed Ellabelle's chest of knowledge was filled entirely with what she'd learned from watching television shows.

For a few moments, Mae Lee was lost in thought. Indeed, she was a little disturbed that she could blame her daughter, with all the unhappiness she was going through. Dallace was struggling under a load of problems too heavy for her to face alone at her age. She knew all too well how much Dallace needed her counsel—far and beyond what she even realized. It didn't matter that Dallace was over forty now; in the mothering department there are no age limits.

She had been startled, but not overly saddened, by her daughter's decision to divorce her husband. When Dallace told her about the child's picture she'd accidentally found in her husband's wallet, Mae Lee wished she'd been more understanding, more so than her mama, Vergie, had been with her. But she'd been angry, angry that her daughter in all her years of marriage had considered herself too proper and high-class to look through her husband's wallet every now and then. That was just one more form of the night work a wife had to perform. All she had to do was not have a headache, and she would be sure of a free chance to search his pockets and wallet when he fell asleep. Her mama had taught her all those kind of things long ago. But back then, daughters listened to their mamas.

Even if she had told her, Mae Lee didn't believe her daughter would have listened. Her guarded daughter was, after all, Dr. Dallace Wallace, a professional person who claimed she always respected a person's privacy. So she'd found the picture only when her husband asked her to hand him his wallet and it fell out, a picture of a little boy whose Asian heritage could not be denied, nor could it disguise the genes of her husband.

When she confronted him, he readily admitted that, yes, that was his son. Mae Lee thought of her grandchildren, the mental image of the missing-tooth smile of her pretty, ponytailed granddaughter, Shella, and the impish grin of her little Tread, with his second-growth of buckteeth, flashed before her.

Lately Mae Lee's daughters had always been reminding her that her thinking was not on the "same page" as theirs. Well, in that case she wanted to tell her daughters that on her "page," and on the same for her friends, the child was a "you-know-what." In her eyes the father was no longer married to her daughter. As far as she was concerned, her daughter's marriage had ended when her husband slept outside his marriage bed. This is the eighties, she wanted to say; be a smart young woman.

She wanted personally to hurt her son-in-law for what he'd said to her daughter Dallace about the braces that were so badly needed for his son Tread's teeth. He had said that the money spent on the outside son was better served. After all, he didn't want to alter their son's looks; "He's a spitting image of his old man," he had laughed, adding with a roguish wink, "he'll have some pretty young thing as wild over him as you are over me."

It pained her that in recent years her precious daughter

had been hanging on to such worthless trash. Changing to crazy hairstyles, spreading layers of makeup on her face, as if she were competing with a seven-layer pineapple cake, and of course there were the miniskirts. A wife trying to force a chaser of miniskirted females to turn around and chase her. Dallace's saving grace was her legs; she had great legs, legs like her mama's.

Poor Dallace. It didn't matter that she had "doctor" before her name, or "Ph.D." after it, or wherever they put it. She was a pitiful woman. Dallace had been stricken with a "mother's affliction," thorns in a mother's side. Mae Lee wanted so desperately to gather her child and grandchildren to her side, and give them the down-home grandma comforts, sunshine-fresh ironed sheets that smelled of the fragrant lilac talcum powder she always sprinkled on mattress covers; her home cooking; long hours on the front porch.

Ellabelle offered more advice. "Remember, when we were coming along we did plenty, plenty of stuff that would have worried our parents to death, but we turned out all right."

"Speak for yourself," Mae Lee retorted. But then she relented. "It's true," she finally agreed. "But for the most part they didn't know about it. I wonder which is better, to know or not to know? I think not knowing keeps your hair black longer."

"Or else, not allow a gray hair in the county and do like you're doing, buying out the drugstore to cover the gray," laughed Ellabelle. She slapped her arm; a whining mosquito raised itself. "These mean old boogers are starting to act nasty. They say only the females bite. That figures. Guess I'll head home and turn in. Oh, Lordy," she groaned, "I can tell I'm getting old. I'm starting to get pains where I didn't even know I had a place."

"You're going to end up on a kidney machine if you don't start drinking more water. The only liquid you get comes from a can."

"How do you know that all I drink is soft drinks?"

"It's all I ever see you drink. I don't believe you can swallow water. You even take your blood pressure pills with Pepsi."

"Well," Ellabelle said, "you won't have to worry about it no more. I'll never bring my cans of soda again. Not as long as I live on the face of this earth. You are sitting here talking behind my back. I can't stand that."

"Ellabelle, we are face to face," Mae Lee reminded her.

When they finished laughing, Ellabelle said, "I've been aiming to tell you I saw Fred Rivers's widow the other day. She's nothing but skin and bones. Going down fast, she's going to worry herself to death over. . . ." Her voice trailed off. "I know where we all need to take our problems. I know exactly where I'm taking mine."

Mae Lee grunted, thinking, if you're planning on taking them to the Lord tonight, be prepared to wait a spell for help. Because with just the calls coming in from Rising Ridge alone, I don't think he could handle them, even with "call waiting."

Part : IV

: 11 :

One spring afternoon in 1987, Mae Lee's son, Taylor, made her aware that there was a world beyond her front porch.

Having suffered a badly wounded knee and leg during the war, he was eternally grateful for hospital volunteers, and now he urged her to make the decision to volunteer down at the hospital.

"Mama," he coaxed, "you need to get out and do things. You're too intelligent to sit around all day and do nothing worthwhile. If you aren't careful, you are going to front-porch yourself to death."

"Strange, my girls don't feel I'm all that intelligent."

"What do they know?"

"They know I wouldn't fit in with all the white ladies down there. That's what they know."

Mae Lee thought of the countless hours when she did nothing but while away the afternoons on her front porch, the hours of meaningless talk with Ellabelle that all too often turned to mean gossiping. Maybe that was why she was beginning to think her mind was slipping away. Maybe since she wasn't using it, the old mind may have thought she didn't need it anymore. Maybe she did have too much free time to think and worry. She'd always known that a person should keep busy.

She smoothed a few strands of hair back from her forehead and fanned her face a little. "I've never done anything like that before, son. Besides, I don't know any of the ladies down at the hospital," she said.

"That's the least that should hold you back, Mama. You've never met a stranger in your life," Taylor said.

Mae Lee shook her head. "I don't know if it would work for me. It would sort of be like moving next door to Mrs. Grant, in that rich neighborhood she lives in."

Taylor swirled the ice in his tea around and around—clink, clink. His mama watched him knit his brows in a worried frown, his jaws moving in a seesaw fashion. She shook her head. "Stop gritting your teeth, son."

He flashed a broad grin. His mama stared. He was so good-looking, it was pitiful. Looked so much like his daddy it hurt.

"What you thinking about, baby?" she asked after a minute.

"Thinking about what you said. How you probably wouldn't fit in at the hospital." Taylor was dead serious. "Lots of black women are volunteers at hospitals."

"Not in Rising Ridge, South Carolina."

Taylor frowned.

"Name one, just one," she urged.

"Well, maybe I can't," he sighed, "but, Mama, they need to
126

be. Somebody's got to be first. First in Rising Ridge, that is. When I was in the hospital in San Francisco, the hospital volunteers were black as well as white there. And oh, Mama, I can't put into words how much they meant to me. Think of all the children in the hospital. And Mama, you know in that department we have our share. As far as handling things, you can handle any situation that comes up. Just handle it the way you handle us. By the time you're finishing up with your guilt salve, they'll come around."

Mae Lee showed her surprise, "What do you know about guilt grease, child?"

"Same as I know about everything else. The instructions on how to apply it don't read For Use by Women Only. The ointment can work both ways."

"Taylor, we are talking about old-timey stuff here. I haven't heard guilt salve mentioned since my mama died."

"My mother-in-law said that she heard you say, 'If you want to make someone do something, just rub a little guilt on them just like you would rub on some ointment,'" Taylor laughed. "She shouldn't have told me that in front of Bettina. Now I'll know what she's trying to pull on me. Bettina can't bring me to *my* knees, trying to lay on guilt."

"You shouldn't give her cause to try," Mae Lee opened her refrigerator. "You want a slice of egg custard?"

"Oh, yes, ma'am!"

Mae Lee sliced the pie. She couldn't get her son's mother-in-law out of her mind. How dare that old gray biddy share that kind of information with a man as young as Taylor! A young married man doesn't need to know that sort of thing. If he ever starts to chase skirts, which he may have already, his wife won't have any kind of tool to settle him down with. Taylor is a married man, so let him be saddled with guilt when he needs it. If and when he deserves it, let his wife lay it on him.

"That was my mama's secret," she said aloud.

"I know," her son said, cramming more custard into his full mouth. Taylor thought she was talking about the pie. He wiped his mouth with the back of his hand, then drew in a deep breath through his nose, Andy Griffith–style, saying, "But yours is better."

Mae Lee drew a deep breath. Whew!

Taylor leaned back in his chair, his hands clasped behind his head. "I wonder, when things come out in the newspaper about your volunteer work at the hospital, if they'll mention your pies? It's kind of nice when you read in the paper about the fine jobs the ladies are doing—people helping people, PHP."

His mama showed interest. "I guess it is nice to be able to read about yourself in the newspaper when you haven't killed somebody or else died. I'm right certain I'll be on some page in the newspaper even if the death notice page is full. Elisha Frazier always makes sure everybody he handles gets a notice run in the paper." She sighed. "I guess they'll get me. My body that is. I've been keeping up a burial policy with the Frazier Funeral Home for mighty near forty years."

In many ways Mae Lee could agree with Taylor about the hospital, but her favorite place was really at home. It was a good feeling to get up and not be forced to go to work on a job. Some of her friends still had to do that. She would never forget the rotating shifts at the munitions plant. The memory of having to get up in the middle of the night and go to work still tore into her sleep.

She liked being home, liked having company. That's why she still had an insurance man come to collect on her burial premium. At least the young man was someone she could safely invite inside. She knew him. Mostly she loved getting out her checkbook, writing, with no embarrassment, sixty-five-cent checks. "My children," she would say, soothing the back of her hand, "always see to it that I keep a little something in my checking account."

Taylor's little speech stuck in her craw, however. It nibbled on her conscience. So many people couldn't help themselves; so many needed help. Suppose, just suppose, that was why she had been given her health and strength. If she didn't use it rightly, maybe it might be taken away. It was a troubling thought.

Taylor had watched his mama's eyes narrow into that searing "I know what you got on your tongue and you'd better not let it slide off" look, and had changed his course in his little prepared speech. Once when he had chided his nonworking wife and her mama about never volunteering for anything unless there was food there, he had gotten into trouble. His mother-in-law had hotly retorted that the reason that she and a lot of others were not down at the Red Cross and places like that was because most of them were already doing volunteer work—taking care of their grandchildren.

Mae Lee watched her son leave, his body straight and tall. There was not the slightest trace of a limp. She said aloud,

"Someone, probably some mother, perhaps with a more busy life than mine, still made the time to reach out and help him when he was in the hospital. Someone helped my Taylor."

When Taylor got to his car, he turned, "Oh, by the way, I forgot to ask if you'll keep the kids for us next Saturday and Sunday, Mama?"

She scratched her head, "I'm not sure I'll be free that weekend, honey—but I guess I could always cancel." She waved him on. "And you didn't forget, either. It just took you that long to get up enough nerve to ask."

Mae Lee laughed aloud when her son Taylor drove away. Among her friends, she believed she was the only grandmother over sixty-two years old who wasn't a taken-for-granted, built-in baby-sitter.

When Taylor came to pick up his children Sunday afternoon he didn't ask if she'd gone down to the hospital. Instead he invited his mama to watch the Atlanta Braves play on television with him. "If I don't watch it here," he'd said, "I'll miss it by the time I get home."

"Oh, damn, damn," Taylor yelled when a runner trying to steal a base was tagged out.

"Don't cuss, Taylor," his mama said.

"The Braves make me cuss," Taylor said. "If there's a new way to lose, they'll always come up with it. They're two runs back, and they got Simmons at the plate with Murphy following, and nobody out, so they send the runner and he gets thrown out. Makes no sense."

Mae Lee watched as the next batter, a big, heavy-shouldered

man, hit the ball out of the park, and the crowd roared. "See what I mean?" Taylor said. "If they hadn't sent that runner, the game would be all even now!"

The next batter, a tall, thin man, also hit a home run, which sent Taylor leaping to his feet. "They're tied up! Hot damn!"

"Taylor! What did I tell you about cussing?" But Mae Lee was interested now. She settled in to watch the game, which the Braves ended up winning. The next afternoon she turned on the television and watched the game on her own.

A few days later Mae Lee made up her mind to check into volunteering at the hospital. She decided to make a phone call instead of going there. She could be much braver on the phone. She held on until she was transferred to the proper office. Secretly she hoped they wouldn't need anyone. Then she could tell her son that she had tried.

The woman she spoke with sounded pleased that she wanted to help. "We always need volunteers," she said. When she learned who Mae Lee was, she sounded genuinely pleased that she would come. "I remember your mama so well. She was a fine woman. When can you start, Mrs. Barnes? I am so anxious to meet you."

The next morning Mae Lee walked into the lobby and slowly approached the information desk. It became clear she had been expected. Within a few minutes, women in pink jackets surrounded her. She could see why they were sometimes called "Pink Ladies." They seem friendly enough, she thought, but then, as Taylor had said, "They are people helping people."

Mae Lee studied the group, trim and alert women who

no doubt had grapefruit, toast, and coffee for breakfast, and nibbled on thin lettuce sandwiches for lunch. The blond and auburn-haired women were very much like her—badly in need of a dye touch-up job. Most of the women were about her age, she guessed, but then, with white women it was hard to tell. At least it was for her.

Hearing them talk, Mae Lee decided that most of them had someone working in their homes. Women with rings like they had on their fingers don't clean houses. Bethel Petty, a tall, striking woman with a face and body that seemed too young for her soft white hair, showed Mae Lee around and explained some of the things the volunteers did. They delivered flowers, mail, and newspapers to the patients' rooms, filled bedside water pitchers, and assisted in delivering meals.

Mae Lee couldn't help thinking how strange it was that so many women living so near her in the same little town could be such total strangers to her. Despite the fact that the town was now fully "integrated," blacks and whites still lived in different circles socially. And religiously; during the weekdays there was mixing and blending, but come Sunday morning the green light changed to a red light that held its steady signal until the worship hours ended. It was all a matter of custom, a holdover from a time when there wasn't even a thought on the part of either race, white or black, of invading the territory of the other. Today, except for an occasional rare visit, blacks still attended black churches, and whites, white churches. The old saying "Birds of a feather flock together" was still true.

Taylor had been so right. Volunteers were very much needed at the hospital. One day when they were short of volunteers, there was a school bus accident in which a number of children were injured. That day Mae Lee and Bethel Petty took turns escorting patients to and from X ray and answering the ringing phones. They didn't even get a coffee break. It was almost time for dinner before some patients received their midafternoon juice.

After a few weeks, it surprised Mae Lee that in spite of the long hours she sometimes spent at the hospital she still had so much free time on hand. She'd signed up to work two days a week, but soon put in to be called for additional days if they were short of help.

She was starting to enjoy working with the rotating group there. They may not have had any thoughts about her side of town, but Mae Lee certainly thought about theirs, and the weddings, garden parties, and cucumber sandwiches that made the Rising Ridge *Chronicle*'s society page.

She was intensely curious about the breakup of the marriage of a man, Stroud Collier. So was everyone else. Everyone wondered why the son of the wealthiest family in town had married the pretty daughter of the second wealthiest, and then got their marriage annulled. Honeymoon one night, marriage ended the next. It did seem strange that someone could love a person enough to marry, and then fall out of love so quickly. There were women in Mae Lee's little section of town who worked in the homes of both families, and who had quickly enough come up with an answer. "Stroud Collier," they said, "had bought a pig in a poke. It was as simple as that." Marylove Redding may have been as pretty as any movie star, but in bed looks don't mean nothing to a man.

The women at the hospital were also talking about Stroud

Collier. Mae Lee didn't turn from untying newspapers, but she listened with open ears. One of the women said, "I heard from a very reliable source that it was the groom, not the bride, who ended the marriage. And, no one, except the two of them, knows the reason, not even their parents." The women from "down where the dirt road begins" probably hadn't been too far off, Mae Lee decided. Money sure can't fix everything, she thought.

"He probably found out something he didn't know," someone else said. "Men don't like some surprises."

You know how you women are, Mae Lee wanted to say. You feel so pressed upon to tell the man you love everything, and when you get a ring on your finger you bare your pitiful little souls. Even if he's your husband, all a man needs to know is what he already knows. And sometimes that's too much.

The one named Melanie Findley glanced at her watch. "I've got to run. I have to deliver supplies to the emergency room," she said.

The other white ladies talked on. "Well, at any rate, Stroud Collier didn't like what he found. Maybe he didn't find her to be a real person. I believe he always liked things pure and real."

Mae Lee couldn't hold her thoughts any longer. She broke the silence. "So real," she said, "that he never thought about himself. From all I hear, Stroud Collier was no saint. And if I knew it, so did everyone else. If his new bride hadn't opened up her little foolish heart on their wedding night they'd probably still be married, with a baby on the way." She heaved a sigh. "Why can't women learn that when it comes to marriage and sex, men are blind? Poor things, they only know to eat what they are fed."

The ladies were silent for a moment. Have I shocked them? Mae Lee wondered. Well, it was true, even so—not that she had any real right to tell other women how to keep a man. Her own marriage didn't even last ten years.

"My husband knew everything about me, because I told him," a small blond volunteer put in. And Mae Lee thought to herself, yes, and that's why, like me, you're a grass widow today. At least my husband didn't carry with him the knowledge of my entire life.

"Maybe Mae Lee is right about not telling everything," Fran Bratton giggled. "I have a friend whose husband worships the ground she walks on. She tells him nothing about anything. But from the moment she met him, whenever she is in his presence she locks her big, wide-set, crystal-clear, china-blue eyes into a 'you-are-so-wonderful' gaze. I'm not commenting on the look she gives when he is out of sight. Her poor dear husband is so wonderfully gullible."

"I guess we could learn a thing or two from her," Bethel Petty said. The ladies broke into laughter.

Mae Lee could see that the ladies made no attempt to conceal their delight over the breakup of Stroud Collier's marriage. She couldn't help but think it was because it put Stroud Collier's card back into the deck again, giving their own daughters yet another chance.

She came to decide that her work down at the hospital pleased Ellabelle even more than it did her children. On the

135

days she worked, Ellabelle would be waiting for her return, often with a covered dish of something she'd baked or cooked.

On one of the days when Mae Lee was especially tired, Ellabelle said, "I want to know about everything that went on down there today, every single word they said."

"If you want to know what goes on down at the hospital so badly, then you ought to volunteer, Ellabelle. It would do you good," she'd snapped.

Ellabelle looked hurt at her friend's cutting words. "I know they need help down there," she said quietly, "but I've got to get my smile fixed first. It costs something to sit in a dentist's chair these days." For a few days, Ellabelle didn't visit her. Mae Lee was concerned and called. Ellabelle didn't offer any reason for not visiting. She simply said, "I'll see you sometime." Mae Lee forced herself not to question her friend. When Ellabelle did show up again, she claimed she couldn't stay, just needed to borrow a little money. "Twenty-five dollars if you have it," she'd said.

Mae Lee searched in her purse. "Twenty is all I have on me."

Ellabelle grinned. "Just checking to see if you're still my friend. I don't need any money. I just got my check yesterday." She settled in a comfortable chair. "So tell me what's new." Things were back to normal, and the gossip pot set to boil again.

"The news is, I'm going to stop telling them anything. I'm going to seal my lips. Especially when Bethel Petty is around. The one I call 'the Professor.' You know who I mean?"

Ellabelle nodded.

"She bothers me. Remember the time a group of us went

down to Myrtle Beach in your son's van? Well, I was telling them how I loved listening to the waves come in and splash up on the sandy beach. I told them how I made your son stay on into the night, just so I could listen to the roar of the waves one after another, like they were timing themselves. And of course the Professor had to up and say—'Oh these waves are nothing. You should hear them in California, where they're much bigger. You see, the wind blows from west to east, and the waves out there have traveled all the way across the Pacific Ocean.'"

It wasn't really what Bethel Petty had said about the waves that bothered Mae Lee, however. It was what she'd said about Africa and the Atlantic Ocean. Years ago Mae Lee's daddy had told her to try and make her way to the Atlantic Ocean if she could, and when she did to pick up anything she could that might have washed ashore, because just by chance she might pick up some trace of heritage—her roots.

Her daddy had said it was his guess that no one could accurately measure the length of time it might take something to travel thousands of miles across the ocean from Africa, swishing and churning around in the bowels of the mighty Atlantic Ocean, before it reached South Carolina, or how many journeys it would have to make before it was washed ashore.

Mae Lee knew by heart the story of how her great-great-grandfather, standing on the shores of the Atlantic Ocean in Africa, had held onto his father's leg. His father had grabbed hold of his son's hand and had refused to let it go. So they sailed and survived the Atlantic together, and landed on South Carolina's shores.

And so Mae Lee had stood there down in Myrtle Beach, South Carolina, less than one hundred and fifty miles from where she was born and raised, gazing at the ocean. Her eyes searched the sandy shores, for what she did not know. She felt if she saw what she was looking for, then she would know. She saw hundreds of seashells, but she didn't collect a single one. One day, she vowed, she would return to continue her search. She would never abandon it.

And then the Professor riddled her hopes with tiny holes. "Are you sure of the likelihood of something leaving the shores of Africa ending up on the shores of South Carolina?" she'd asked. "In my thinking it would probably end up somewhere else, because of the flow of the ocean current."

Mae Lee looked long and hard at Bethel Petty before she said anything. I'll just use a little guilt salve here, she thought to herself. She felt put down. She had just assumed that anything leaving Africa would somehow be washed ashore in South Carolina. She could feel the anger within her rise. This is why I tried to tell my son I didn't want to be down here, she thought.

Finally, she said, "All I know and do understand is that there was something the undercurrent did carry and cause to surface here, and that was the slave ship that brought my fore-fathers. It sailed the Atlantic and reached the shores of South Carolina."

She couldn't believe afterward that she had then turned right around and blurted out that her Indian heritage was also difficult to trace. "What tribe?" Bethel Petty asked. Come to think of it, she couldn't remember ever hearing anyone say.

All her life it had simply been said there was Indian blood in the family. Most people had accepted that. But she truly didn't know what tribe.

When she was pushed against a wall, Mae Lee always thought of water. She thought of the largest body of water she'd seen before viewing the Atlantic Ocean. "Catawba," she said. The Catawba River was part of her. She remembered how, so often, when the warm nights heated the water, steam vapors would rise like smoke in the early morning. Then the river looked like it was on fire.

Before she could finish, the Professor had seized upon it and finished her sentence. "Oh, yes," she chimed in, "the Catawba. I read recently that those native Americans still get clay from the banks of the Catawba River to make their pottery."

Mae Lee started to fan. Sidestepping the truth was hot work. Really hot. In the future, she told herself, she would make her words few. If you said one single word to them, they'd turn it into a thousand. A group of white women was very much like a country well. A bucket goes down empty, comes up full. Privately, Mae Lee made the decision that she would still look to the mighty Atlantic to wash up some clues to help her trace her heritage.

It pleased her that later in the day, when the ladies gathered for cake someone sent in for them, Bethel Petty pulled out her pictures she'd shown the day before and made the ladies crow over them all over again. Bethel Petty had actually forgotten having done something!

Ellabelle bristled. "I don't think I could stand her. I believe I'd have to lay something on that white woman."

Mae Lee drew a long breath. "At first I thought I couldn't stand her, either. But I work side by side with Bethel Petty down at the hospital, and it's kind of hard not to like an honest person. I've accepted an invitation for a dinner party next month and Bethel Petty will be there."

Ellabelle looked at Mae Lee. "Now you are going to have to make up some excuse why you are not going to that dinner party or whatever it is. If I were you, I wouldn't set foot in any one of their houses."

Mae Lee studied the scars on her fingers. She remembered how every single one got there. A couple of scars were from the sharp, pointed edges of open cotton bolls that had ripped her skin open, the others were from welding burns when she worked at the munitions plant.

She looked Ellabelle squarely in the eyes. "I'm going," she said firmly, "and I am going to hold my china teacup with my pinkie finger sticking out." She rocked her body from side to side. "I would even go if Bethel Petty was giving the party. They're not going to keep me away."

Ellabelle anchored an elbow on her thigh, cupped her chin on the curved finger of a half-opened fist, and gazed into the distance. "I've said all I have to say about your coworker, Miss Bethel."

Mae Lee sighed heavily, and rocked some more. "Bethel Petty has some good qualities, in spite of her mouth, but sometimes with her know-it-all self, she's really insensitive. When I eyed her and told her about the Atlantic undercurrent flow not preventing the slaves from Africa ending up in South Carolina, she just looked at me. 'Mae Lee,' she said, 'I am sick and tired of people draping a mantle of guilt around my shoulders for something I didn't do. I had nothing to do with bringing the slaves from Africa to South Carolina.'"

"I couldn't honestly let her get away with it, Ellabelle, I had to say, 'I know you didn't, Bethel, but I bet your family paid your cook four dollars a week and totes.'"

"What did she say to that?" Ellabelle asked.

"She didn't say anything at first. Then she said, 'We probably did, Mae Lee. That was the going rate. We just didn't understand. Nobody did. We were being unfair, and we didn't even realize that we were. I hope we've learned better, most of us.'"

Mae Lee was silent. "They are good people," she said finally. "They do their best. I can say one thing about Bethel, she is plenty smart."

"Humph," Ellabelle grunted.

Perhaps the single thing that bothered Mae Lee most about the ladies in the hospital group was their notion that she knew every black person in the county. She didn't. True, she did know who most of the black patients' people were, but usually the patients themselves were not personal acquaintances.

Bethel Petty must have asked her a dozen times if she knew Sally Jean and Tirzah Davis. She did know *them*, all right, and if she didn't, she would have come to know them anyway. At least one of their children wound up in the hospital every single week. There were nine of those children, but neither parent had a job, so it seemed they should have had time to take better care of them than they obviously did.

The last time one of the children entered the hospital, it was said that when the doctor asked the poor little fellow how often he had the stomachache he was complaining about, the little boy said, "Every time I get hungry, and that's a lot of the times."

When the group invited her to go with them to deliver the food package they had collected, Mae Lee's heart sank. The day the food was to be delivered, Mae Lee paid an early morning visit to the Davis house to help get the place halfway cleaned up. It was midafternoon when she left. She was so weary that every step she made was a painful effort, and even though she was nearly home she still accepted a ride from Ellabelle when she stopped her car.

"You look like something the cat dragged home," Ellabelle said.

Mae Lee closed the car door. "I am so-oo tired."

"I didn't know you went down to the hospital on Wednesdays. I could have picked you up, if you weren't too proud to let somebody know your comings and goings," Ellabelle fussed. She stopped at Mae Lee's house but Mae Lee didn't get out right away.

"I'm just too tired to move for a minute yet. I didn't go to the hospital today. I went over to Sally Jean's early this morning," she said.

"Oh, is she sick again?"

"No, she's all right now. Remember I told you they brought her into the emergency room a few weeks ago for chest pains?"

Ellabelle laughed. "Yes, I remember, it was the night she ate all those roasted peanuts and cooked cabbage and ended up with terrible indigestion. But then, if she hadn't been there it would have been one of her kids. I think they take turns getting hurt so the family won't miss a week at the hospital." Ellabelle frowned. "If no one was sick why did you go?"

"Well, some of the women down at the hospital got together some goodies for the kids and were taking them over today. So I went over early."

Ellabelle shook her head. "I kind of believe I'd have been ashamed to be there when the women from the hospital visited. You know for yourself Sally Jean's not much of a house-keeper."

Mae Lee opened the car door and got out. Before she closed the door she told Ellabelle, "Her house was spic-and-span when the hospital volunteers got there."

"Well, it's the first time it's ever been," Ellabelle said acidly, and drove off.

: 12 :

Bethel Petty wasn't intentionally rude or dismissive, but she had a way of saying things that could be annoying, and sometimes even upsetting, as in her remark about the navy blue jacket. Mae Lee wore the jacket on a damp morning when it was a bit too cool to go out without one. It looked quite nice over the pearl gray blouse she'd bought at a yard sale the Saturday before.

Bethel Petty was hard at work on the volunteer schedule when Mae Lee walked in. She spoke but didn't look up. "Thanks for totaling up the hours for the volunteer report, Mae Lee," she said. "It's sad that the more the workload for the doctors and nurses increases, the more the hours of the volunteer group decrease. I see that Deborah Ross is having out-of-town company next Tuesday. Do you think you could switch your day next week with her?" She looked up, and before Mae Lee could answer, the woman started, got up, moved

144

forward, and lightly ran her fingers along the jacket sleeve. "Um, nice," she said, adding, "good Ultrasuede. Where did you get it?"

Mae Lee, obviously pleased, answered, "One of my daughters sent it to me."

"Which one?"

"Nellie Grace."

Bethel raised her eyebrows, "Oh, the one who drives the new BMW. My Lord, Mae Lee, what in the world does your daughter *do* to earn that kind of money?"

Mae Lee read doubts in Bethel Petty's eyes, and simply answered, "Nellie Grace was recently divorced, and in her words, won a very generous settlement and she has a *very* good job." She thought to herself, "She's a computer specialist, but you will not get me out on a limb trying to go into details, Professor." Then she began to think about it. She thought of the time she'd visited her daughter in New York, thought of all the nice things in her apartment. She started mentally adding up all the things her daughter had bought that Bethel Petty didn't even know about.

It was troubling to have someone question the conduct of her child. It worked on her nerves.

The workday seemed to stretch on forever, but she doggedly pressed on to the end. That evening she was getting ready to start cooking supper when Ellabelle called to say she was bringing over a freshly baked beef casserole. It was one of Mae Lee's favorite dishes, but this time she only picked at the food.

"Something is bothering you, Mae Lee," Ellabelle said. "You don't look sick, but when you can't eat, something is bad wrong. What happened today to set you off?"

Mae Lee frowned. "I guess it was the way Bethel Petty talked about Nellie Grace's car and the clothes she sent me. It was kind of like nobody could afford such fine things from just the money they are paid on their jobs. She wanted to know 'what in the world' my child did for a living."

Ellabelle pulled both feet upon the chair rung. Mercifully it didn't break. She slapped her thighs hard and clenched her fists. "Damn that woman! I've worked around Them long enough to know how They think. As soon as They see us come up in life and get a little something, if we are not in sports or entertainers the first thing they think is that we are doing something crooked."

Mae Lee seemed lost in thought. She finally broke the silence. "Times are changing for our children. Slowly, but surely. And we are changing with it. A lot of us are getting our feet on solid ground."

"The women down at the hospital need to know that," Ellabelle put in. "That's what I'm thinking. They need to know that."

Mae Lee turned in her chair to face Ellabelle. "Bethel Petty needs to know that, and yes, I do need to tell her, and I will."

Ellabelle looked at Mae Lee. "I sure wouldn't go out of my way to do it, though. Like I said before, I'd be hard-pressed to go to an old party that They invited me to."

It was all very well for Ellabelle to say that Mae Lee shouldn't go to the party. Ellabelle didn't work with the ladies at the hospital three and four days a week, and didn't sit around with them talking about families and children and people and events in town. These people had become her *friends,* some of them. Certainly they occasionally said things that they didn't realize could be awkward and embarrassing to her. But it wasn't because they meant them that way. They didn't always understand. And as far as she was concerned, the job was to make them understand, help them to understand. If she were to allow little things, unintentional things, like that to keep her from being part of the group, when everybody concerned, including Bethel Petty, *wanted* her to be part of it, then they would never, ever learn to understand. She, Mae Lee Barnes, was tired of other people telling her what she should and should not do. She wanted to go to the party, and they wanted her to come to the party. They really did. So she was going to go to the party.

On the Saturday of the dinner party, Mae Lee woke long before daylight. She couldn't go back to sleep, but she stayed in bed for a while anyway. For the rest of the day she was so busy pulling out dresses and shoes, trying to decide what to wear, that she didn't even think about how nervous she was becoming.

In the evening, Ellabelle drove Mae Lee to Margaret Wade's house. "Have a good time," Ellabelle said, "and don't worry too much over missing the Atlanta Braves game tonight."

Mae Lee made a weak smile. "Be sure to let me know if the Braves win."

As soon as she walked inside the house, Bethel Petty loudly

announced, "Mae Lee's here!" Mae Lee glanced about the room, her thoughts confirmed. Just as she'd suspected, there was only one black person there, at least in that room—herself. At first she felt a bit uneasy, but it passed when Deborah Collins rushed to her side. "Oh, Mae Lee," she began excitedly, "let me tell you what happened down at the hospital yesterday. Remember the patient in Room 103?"

Mae Lee smiled. "Good old Mr. Rayburn?"

"Yes, here's what happened. He decided he was going home, and guess what? He made it all the way to the front door with nothing on but his hospital gown and his medical bracelet before anyone noticed that he had left his room. The poor dear man stood there at the door—" Deborah blushed, "—with his gown wide open in the back." She shook her head, "I would have died, Mae Lee, if I'd been working on the first floor and let that happen."

Mae Lee hadn't been the least bit hungry when she left home, but when she tasted the fork-tender roast beef and the angel biscuits, her appetite returned.

"No wonder they call them angel biscuits; they are heavenly," Linda Salter said.

Margaret Wade smiled, "Theldocia Sampson made them. She makes the best biscuits in the world."

I should have known one of us was in the kitchen, Mae Lee thought. Otherwise the food would have never tasted this good. Mae Lee knew Theldocia, but didn't know that she cooked for the Wades. At least Margaret Wade had called her by her last name as well as her first.

Mae Lee also thought that if Margaret Wade didn't put away

the big, porcelain, kerchief-clad, red-lipped black mammy doll in her kitchen cupboard, Theldocia would be sure to just happen to break it into a million pieces one day, then moan ever so pitifully, "Oh, Lord have mercy, Miss Wade, I sure didn't aim to break it. Maybe we can glue her back together." Mae Lee had spotted the doll right in front of the dishes when Margaret Wade opened the cabinet for a small plate. She had then glanced at Mae Lee standing there and closed the door so quickly she didn't even take the time to remove a plate. Later Mae Lee wished she could have thought to say "Gotcha."

Mae Lee stayed on for quite some time with her hospital friends.

"I wonder how old Mr. Jonas is doing today?" Mabel Griffin remarked. "He was having trouble after all that surgery on his knee."

"He's got to learn to use his walker," Ellen Smith said. "He's awfully impatient, you know."

"He was walking fine yesterday afternoon," Mae Lee told them. "He went all the way down the hall and back."

"Did you have to help him?" Ellen Smith asked.

"Just a little. He couldn't turn himself around too good. But once he got himself lined up he was all right."

"I wish," Helen Davis declared, "that Dr. Jervey could be a little more patient sometimes when he tells them how to use the walker. He doesn't realize how hard it is for some people to adapt to using one. Especially if they've had hip surgery."

"You're right," Mae Lee agreed. "Sometimes I feel like telling that man, you just slow up now, and make sure they really understand what you're telling them. You might think there's nothing to it, but they've never done it before, or even thought about doing it until now!"

"Of course we mustn't *dare* criticize the medical staff, you know," Mabel Griffin said. "Never, no never!"

Everybody laughed. "Well, I'd certainly like to criticize them sometimes," Helen Davis agreed.

They talked about the different staff doctors, and other things, the same things they usually talked about at work. Helen Davis remarked that she and her husband were driving to Atlanta for the weekend to see the Braves play. It turned out that Bethel Petty was an expert on that subject, too. "They're playing the Cubs this weekend," she declared, "so maybe they can win two games in a row for a change. If they can only score lots of runs, that is. They lose all the close games."

"That's what my son says, too," Mae Lee said. "He says whenever they have to go to the bullpen it's all over."

"Your son's absolutely right," agreed Bethel Petty.

: 13 :

It was July. Outside beyond the cool corridors of the hospital the weather was blazing hot. Jeanne Nelson asked Mae Lee to work in the gift shop while she went for a cup of tea. "It's that English part of me," she explained once.

It was alien to Mae Lee how anyone could even think of hot tea on a hot summer day.

Then she thought about the lemon sweets her mama had made for her "silver teas." She'd called them lemon biscuits and Mae Lee remembered after all that her mama would serve them with hot tea and homemade ice cream in the summer months, after the farm women finished picking wild blackberries. She would have her home-canned berries, jams, and jellies all in plain sight for the ladies to see. Mae Lee grew up thinking that showing off her efforts was the only reason for the silver tea.

It got Mae Lee to thinking. Since the ladies at the hospital seemed to be so curious about the silver teas, Mae Lee decided to invite them to one. She'd been going to their parties as they gave them, but she had hesitated to give a party of her own. It wasn't that she was afraid of giving a party; she knew she could throw a good one. It was rather that she felt that the hospital ladies would feel obliged to come, whether they wanted to or not, for fear of insulting her. But as she thought about it some more, it seemed to her that it was the same old thing holding her back as before, as if someone somewhere was telling her what *she,* Mae Lee Barnes, ought and ought not to do. If she were not the only black member of the group, wouldn't she have long since given a party for her friends, just as they had invited her to their parties? If so, then why should she allow that to prevent her from taking her turn?

She talked to Taylor about it. "Mama, you're right," he said. "Look at it this way. The only way it's ever going to come to be so that those ladies won't feel they *have* to come to a party when you give it, is for you to start giving parties just like they do. The first time or two it might be a little awkward, but after that nobody will think twice about it. Including you," he added.

Even so, when the day came for the silver tea, she was nervous. It was a blazing hot afternoon, it seemed as if she'd made a deliberate effort to pick the hottest day in the year for it. She'd asked Taylor and his wife, Bettina, and her daughter Annie Ruth to come down and give her a hand.

"I'd ask one of the other girls," she'd said, "but they all live so far away." Still, Annie Ruth asked her sister Amberlee to come anyway. They all hurried about in the midafternoon heat, getting the food ready and tables set up. Mae Lee was nervous, very nervous. She kept biting her lower lip.

"Annie Ruth," she called out, "where is Amberlee? The glass bowls for the ice cream are still in the cupboard."

"Helping Taylor with the ice cream, Mama."

She opened the back screen door. "Amberlee, help Taylor to hurry up and get another churn of ice cream cranked up and going. If I wasn't going to use all those ice-cream churns, I wouldn't have borrowed them. Don't lag behind, children. Taylor, repack that last churn with ice. You didn't allow enough time for it to ripen to suit my taste."

"We're clean out of ice, Mama. Better have somebody run and get some," Taylor called back.

"Somebody help Taylor," she urged her daughters. "Help me get this little silver tea together. When I do something I want it done right. I sure wish I'd made my same strawberry and lemon tarts. I couldn't let myself do what I know how to do best. No, I had to up and show off when I was invited to Their little dinners and parties. I had to say I just *luhhved* to bake, and was even fool enough to claim I always used the same old recipe handed down from my mama for my delicious lemon biscuits. And bragged how my mama used to serve them on summer afternoons with hot tea and homemade ice cream. The truth is, Mama did make the things, but I've never made a lemon biscuit in my life. If I hadn't found that recipe Mama used, I think I would have died."

Annie Ruth shook her head. "Poor Mama."

Mae Lee was near tears. She stood wringing her hands, "How I got myself into a mess like this I'll never know. Only the Lord knows. But if the good Lord pulls me out of this crack, I'll never get into another one, that's for certain."

She remembered her lemon biscuits in the hot oven. She rushed to the stove. They hadn't burned.

"Slow down, Mama," Amberlee urged. "You're gonna mess around and have a stroke. You are putting yourself under too much pressure . . ."

"And us, too," Annie Ruth cut in.

"Mama," Amberlee continued, "you don't need to stress yourself out for that hospital volunteer group. I don't care if they are white women."

"Yes," Annie Ruth agreed, "you never did knock yourself out with anything this fancy for us." She turned to look at Mae Lee. "I hope you told the fancy ladies how to get here, Mama. Take Center Street all the way through town, just short of 'where the dirt road begins' in 'colored town.'"

Amberlee and Bettina laughed.

Mae Lee didn't think it was particularly funny. She turned to Bettina and Annie Ruth struggling to center a cloth on a table. "Annie Ruth, tell your mama that you are not going to put that wrinkled tablecloth on a table. Tell me that you are going to iron it first."

Taylor entered the house and answered a ringing phone. He cupped his hand over the receiver, "Mama, it's Miss Reid. I don't think she's coming. She says she's not feeling well."

Mae Lee wiped her hands and took the phone. "I understand," she repeated, "I understand. Now, if you take a turn for the better, please feel free to come on over at any time, you know you are more than welcome."

She hung up the phone and returned to her cooking. "Bettina," she said, "make some sort of sandwich for Nora Reid.

She'll be here shortly claiming she'll die of hunger if she doesn't put a little something or other in her stomach right away."

"But, Mama Barnes," Bettina protested, "I thought Taylor said Nora Reid was sick."

"Sick, my foot," Mae Lee grunted. "Nora Reid wouldn't miss this silver tea unless she was dead." She smiled, adding, "and you know something, I wouldn't be surprised if even then she'd come. All Nora wanted was for me to beg her. And did you hear me beg? Mae Lee Barnes doesn't beg anyone, for anything!"

Mae Lee put her right hand on her hip and with a folded newspaper softly fanned her face. "If black women are going to mingle socially with white women, you *know* Nora Reid, our proper retired black schoolteacher, will be here trying way too hard to impress, making sure she finds a reason to use every big word she knows. She thinks she's needed because black people won't be properly represented unless she is present."

"African-American, Mama," Annie Ruth corrected.

Mae Lee glared at her daughter and shook her head, "Listen, I'm just barely getting used to black, Annie Ruth."

When Amberlee walked into the kitchen her mother looked over the eyeglasses on her nose and studied her dress. It was the kind of cotton dress that would have been starched, ironed, and worn over a cotton underskirt when she was that age. Now it hung on her daughter's body soft and unironed, topped by hair combed to look a little uncombed.

Mae Lee didn't have to speak her opinion for Amberlee to hear it. "Yes, Mama," she intoned, "things have changed. What you wouldn't have been caught dead in is now downright fashionable."

"You should have at least put on a pair of pantyhose, Amberlee," said Mae Lee.

She glanced out the window at Annie Ruth and Bettina in the yard. They were both bare-legged, with smooth, shaved, hairless legs, like the legs of older women that no longer required shaving.

Amberlee rushed from the kitchen and then back. She pointed to a young man dressed in black, unloading folding chairs from a black hearse. "Mama," she gasped, "he's bringing funeral home chairs to our house!"

Mae Lee gave her youngest child a "so what?" look. "Who else would have that many chairs that matched? Now go round up Annie Ruth and Bettina and tell them to finish setting up before Ellabelle gets here. I don't want her to have to help. Today she's company. Tell them to come into the kitchen as soon as they finish. I have a little gift for each of my girls."

When the daughters were done, Mae Lee proudly handed each one of them a clear plastic bag with the five-dollar "First Lady Pearls" she'd ordered inside. Her daughters exchanged quick glances.

"Well, put them on," Mae Lee urged. "That's why I ordered them. There was a limit—four per address, but since I ordered early, they allowed me to go over the limit. So I ordered one for Bettina. I also ordered me one, too. I still can't get over how much that money order cost."

"Mama, you have a checking account," Annie Ruth asked. "Why didn't you send a check?"

"I forgot where I put my checks. I couldn't find them any-place." She stopped short. "Lordy, Lordy. I forgot all about Ellabelle. I don't always remember her. If Ellabelle asks where you all got your matching three-strand pearls, don't lie—but don't tell her where you got them."

Mae Lee pulled open kitchen cabinets and drawers, search-ing for something. She sighed. "I just tucked my picture pin somewhere a minute ago."

After their mama left the room, Annie Ruth fastened the pearls around Amberlee's neck. "Ellabelle won't even ask, she'll be so glad not to have to wear these," she whispered.

Annie Ruth pointed to pictures on the wall that she had so painstakingly hung at eye level, but now were hung almost up to the ceiling, "What if Mama had fallen off that ladder?"

Amberlee grinned. "I bet you won't find me taking anything down that Mama puts up again. Remember the time the two of us took down the patchwork quilt hanging on the wall at the head of her bed, and she made all five of us, including Taylor, hang it back? She went on about it for a solid week, 'That quilt belonged to my daddy's grandmama. A lot of hard work went into that quilt, mine included, I quilted the border. And just because the colors clashed with some five-and-ten-cent store sheets, one of my daughters takes it down and puts it in a box.'"

"'And I never, ever,'" Annie Ruth added, mimicking her mama, "'want to know for sure which one it was. Of course, I have a pretty good idea that it was Annie Ruth, but I don't want to be absolutely certain, beyond a shadow of doubt. You see, the Lord is my shepherd who watches over me, and I don't want him to see what I might do to my own child, my own flesh and blood if ever I found out.'"

They stopped laughing when Mae Lee entered the kitchen. "I found what I was looking for," she said as she held up her picture pin. She smiled shyly at her daughters and daughter-in-law. "I wonder if this and my first lady pearls would be a bit too much. I'd like to greet my guests with it on."

"Yes, Mama," they all hurriedly agreed. "It would be a bit too much. Actually, much too much."

Mae Lee gazed down at the picture. She was glad it was made before her little Tread had the earring put in his ear. Grudgingly she put the picture pin of her grandson in a drawer.

Taylor brought in a freshly churned container of ice cream to put into the freezer. He took one look at his mother, wife, and sisters, pearl-adorned, grinned, then smothered a laugh when he caught his mother's eye. He read the satisfaction there. "The Bobbsey twins multiplied," he said, smiling broadly.

He turned to his mama. "Miss Reid said you should stop and get a little rest so you'll be refreshed when your guests arrive."

Mae Lee dabbed at the perspiration on her brow with the corner of her apron. "Tell Miss Reid to eat her sandwich. I promise I won't embarrass her." She looked out the window. "I wonder what's keeping Ellabelle and Clairene?" Ellabelle's car was in the shop for repairs and she was coming with her friend Clairene.

"They're coming down the street now," Taylor said, reaching for a lemon biscuit. Mae Lee slapped his hand. "Get back to cranking your churn, child."

Ellabelle met Mae Lee in the kitchen doorway. "Hey, Mae Lee, do you look pretty! I was coming to get you. Your guests are starting to come." She blocked the doorway. "One car just pulled up. Look who's driving Mrs. Wells: that handsome grandson of hers. He's home for the summer. I guess the young women in his circle will go crazy." Amberlee moved to take a look.

"Whoa," she said, "he is drop-dead gorgeous."

Mae Lee watched him open the car door for his grandmother. "He is kind of cute with his no-socks self," she admitted. "But you should have seen his daddy when he was about that age. The man was so good-looking he didn't look real. The talk among the women down at the hospital this week was about how Brandon Wells was coming home from some fancy college in the North. All I can say is as long as he's in town, all of them with daughters had better lock the pasture gates at night."

Mae Lee took off her apron and brushed past Ellabelle to greet her guests. They all arrived within minutes of each other. Mae Lee stood with her children near the front porch steps. She greeted everyone, introducing her family to them, along with Ellabelle, Clairene, and Nora Reid. The ladies began settling into chairs around the tables. There was a certain amount of awkwardness. Mae Lee moved about the group, accepting their compliments on how nice her children looked.

It turned out that Ellabelle and Linda Salter had known each other. "Didn't you work at the munitions plant during the war?" Linda Salter asked.

"I sure did," Ellabelle replied. "Didn't you work in the paymaster's office?"

"Yes indeed!" Linda Salter said. "And you used to come in to pick up the checks for your shift!"

"That's right," Ellabelle laughed. " 'Course I quit early and moved away. Mae Lee was there the whole time, though."

"Oh, Mae Lee," Bethel Petty said, "don't tell me you worked there too?"

It turned out that not only had Mae Lee and Linda Salter and Bethel Petty worked during the war at the shell factory, but so had a half-dozen others, even including Mrs. Wells.

"It's too bad we didn't know each other then," Linda Salter said. The reason they had not, as all present knew only too well, was that the white women mostly had been employed as secretaries and clerical workers, while the black women had been able to get jobs only on the production line or the cleanup crew. Even during the war, they had worked as they had lived, in two different worlds.

It was time to serve the ice cream and tea and lemon biscuits. Mae Lee ushered her children from the porch and into the kitchen. "I guess they *didn't* know each other," Annie Ruth said to Amberlee in a low voice. "How could they have known Mama, when on the bus riding to work and back they couldn't even do something as simple as sitting next to each other to talk?"

"We've been talking about your vegetable garden, Mae Lee,"

Fran Bratton said when Mae Lee returned. "Ellabelle said you do all the work yourself except the plowing. Let me tell you, I haven't seen tomatoes that size since before my daddy died."

Mae Lee laughed. "Well, you must help yourself to some. All of you," she added. "Everyone around here has so many, I can't give them away."

Jeanne Nelson walked to the edge of the porch. "I have tomatoes," she said, "but oh, Mae Lee, I would love a cutting, if it can be done from this beautiful plant. What is it?" She studied the plant's exotic pink flowers. "It's the most beautiful flower I think I've ever seen."

"It's called the hummingbird plant," Mae Lee said. "I'll give you cuttings, they're easy to root."

"Every time someone gives me a cutting it dies on me almost before I get it home," one of the ladies said.

"Maybe it's because you say 'thank you' when it's given to you. The older people used to say that cuttings wouldn't live if you do," Nora Reid answered.

Mae Lee's daughters served helping after helping of Taylor's ice cream and her warm lemon biscuits and poured the tea. Every time the plate was passed, Mary Lou Rice and Pamela Rhoades reached for another biscuit.

"Linda Salter," Melanie Findley called out, "you swore even homemade ice cream couldn't pull you off your diet and now you're on your second helping."

Linda Salter flashed a pretty smile and dropped her head. "I guess I'll just eat crow for supper. Crow again."

Mae Lee was about to comment. Amberlee walked over to her side. "I think your lemon biscuits are burning, Mama," she said, taking her by the arm and pulling her in the direction of the kitchen.

Mae Lee looked over her glasses. "I just put them in the oven." But she went anyway.

"Please, Mama," Amberlee begged, "please don't tell these women how your mama used to cook crow all the time. How she would smother it in brown gravy and cook beaten biscuits to sop up the gravy. Having to 'eat crow' is just a slang expression, Mama. It means you've misspoken, it's like having to eat your words. People really don't *eat crow*."

Mae Lee eased her oven door open for a quick peek at her biscuits. She didn't turn to face her daughter. "We did. And we were lucky to get it sometimes."

"Don't tell those ladies that, Mama, please don't," Amberlee urged. "Not now. Sometime when you're not serving food to them."

Mae Lee started taking dishes down from a cabinet. "Well . . . ," she started, a little smile on her face.

"Oh, Mama, there's that look that never makes me sure if what you've said is true or not," Amberlee groaned.

"Go pick up dirty plates, baby." She waved her daughter from the kitchen, "Shoo, shoo, scat clean out of my kitchen, little pest, out of my way."

It occurred to Mae Lee that she hadn't seen Taylor for a while. "Where's your handsome husband gone to?" she asked Bettina, who was serving cakes to Linda Salter and Mrs. Wells at a table near the side porch.

"Last time I saw him he was out on the side porch," Bettina said. "You know what he's doing out there." She winked.

Mae Lee went out onto the porch. The television set was on, with the Braves game. Taylor was seated in one chair, and in another was Bethel Petty. The two had their backs to her, watching intently.

"Don't throw him a change-up," Taylor said. "Not now."

Mae Lee could recognize who was pitching for Atlanta. She watched as Zane Smith glanced back toward second base, then came in with his pitch. The batter swung and missed.

"What's the score?" Mae Lee asked.

"Three to one Braves, bottom of the seventh," Bethel Petty said without turning her head. "Two out."

When the last guest had said good-bye, Mae Lee plopped into her front porch rocking chair. Ellabelle settled into the porch swing. "I'm too full to go home." She laughed. "I've got to let some of this food digest first."

Taylor laid his hand on his mama's shoulder. "Bettina and I are going to head home now."

Mae Lee leaned her face against his hand. That was usually the extent of Taylor's hug. Taylor had never been a huggy-kissy child. His cousin Warren had teasingly told him he would never grow tall and strong if he let his mother and sisters hug and kiss him all the time and the little boy had believed him. When he was ready to go away to the Vietnam War, his mama had to run down the road after him for a good-bye kiss.

"We pulled off a lot of work, didn't we, Mama?" Taylor said. "Put the two of us together and things get done."

"Look who's talking and taking the credit," Annie Ruth

grumbled. "All Taylor did was pick up the ice and take a few turns hand-cranking the ice cream with Amberlee. There are dirty dishes piled everywhere, but we only heard his wife offer to help. 'We pulled off a lot of work.' We did. Uh huh!"

Ellabelle stood up. "How about dropping me off at my house, Taylor? I'll never make it home on foot."

"Well, it's over," Annie Ruth sighed. "Over and done." She pulled a chair close and put her feet up. "I think, on the whole, They tried to put their best foot forward, Mama. Mrs. Wells thought she was doing you a favor by telling you she couldn't remember a time she'd enjoyed a summer afternoon more."

"Yeah," Amberlee agreed, "and another one even patted Mama on the back by saying she grew tomatoes as good as her own daddy had."

"I guess they had to prove to themselves and each other that they could *so* come and break bread with us people," Bettina said.

"And live to tell about it." Annie Ruth giggled.

"They were on their best behavior for us. Right, Mama?" Amberlee asked.

Mae Lee leaned her head back against the top of her rocker and gazed out into the darkness. "They're no better than colored people," Mae Lee said. "And no worse."

: 14 :

Several days after the August tea party Taylor drove up to his mama's house with airline tickets for Atlanta, Georgia, to see the Braves play. Taylor handed her the tickets and an envelope with money inside. "Everything has been taken care of, Mama," he said. "It's a token of our love. It's from all your children."

She hugged her son. "I don't know how you children ever thought of this."

"It didn't take much doing. Not with you calling every day since the baseball season opened saying how happy you'd be if you could only see the Atlanta Braves play just one baseball game at their stadium in Atlanta."

His mama lowered her head. "One thing I can say for my son, he always speaks his mind. Always has." She leafed through her travel packets. "Looks mighty expensive to me."

She told Ellabelle about the trip to Atlanta. "Go on, girl, go on," Ellabelle sang out.

A few days later, Mae Lee started getting her clothes ready.

She laid her blue hat out on her company bed beside her dress. She looked at the pretty dress with her first lady pearls and a bracelet nearby, and tried to pull in a protruding stomach that would not be pulled. She couldn't figure what in heaven's name was inside her stomach. There wasn't that much fat in the world. It was like she was pregnant again, almost. She had new 'no bulge' gear to wage battle with her body: a waist belt that promised you'd look slimmer instantly. From the same Walter Drake Good Buys mail order insert in the newspaper, she'd also ordered a shoulder brace to combat the effects of stooped shoulders. A brace you would barely know you had on, the advertisement had said. It was true; she'd barely known she had it on, and it also barely helped at all.

On the morning Mae Lee was to make the trip she called her son at six o'clock. She hadn't slept all night. "I'm sorry to call so early," she apologized, "but I am afraid you might oversleep. It's my first plane trip."

"It's all right, Mama," Taylor sleepily answered. "I know."

At the airport she stood out among the crowd of passengers. Clad in the well-placed mantle of dignity belonging to women of a certain age, Mae Lee was anxious even so. "Do my earbobs look all right, Taylor? My skirt isn't twisted, is it?"

Her son assured her she looked fine. "Now that you've started spending time with money people, it's caused you to put your body in a different gear," he said.

For the third time Taylor had to reassure his mama there was no need for her to have fixed a lunch to eat on the plane, even if she didn't like what they served. "It's a short flight, Mama," he said.

"It's my first plane trip," she reminded Taylor yet again. Finally she made her son leave. The waiting was hard for Mae Lee. She watched the passengers and held on to her bags. An elderly man wearing a gold chain and a shirt opened up almost down to his waist moved into a seat across from her. A woman with puffy ankles held tightly to the man's arm, her face reflecting the pain of feet squeezed into brightly colored high-heeled shoes.

When the plane was airborne it leaned to the side and curved to the south. Mae Lee leaned into the window, "Whoa, driver," she said to herself, "straighten this baby up, it's going to flip over."

Soon they were above the clouds. She gazed down on the thick white blanket. It was like a bed of cotton, soft, ginned, seedless cotton. The very thought seemed to relax her. There was an empty seat between Mae Lee and a woman seated next to the aisle. After a little while two stewardesses came along the aisle pushing a cart loaded with drink bottles and cans. "What will you have to drink?" one of the stewardesses asked the woman. "Diet Pepsi," the woman replied. Then she repeated the question to Mae Lee.

"How much does it cost?" Mae Lee asked.

"There's no charge," the stewardess explained.

"I'll have a Diet Pepsi, too," she said.

She watched the woman across from her pull down a little shelf from the back of the facing seat, and she did the same. The stewardess handed her a drink in a plastic cup, and two packages of shelled peanuts.

"This is my first plane trip," Mae Lee explained to the

167

woman. "My children are sending me to Atlanta to see the Braves."

"That's nice," the woman said.

"If it rains tomorrow I don't know what I'll do," Mae Lee said.

"In that case you could watch them over television, couldn't you?" the woman asked.

"Not if it's raining. If it's raining they won't be on television either."

"Really?" the woman said. "What a shame!" How dumb can you be? Mae Lee thought to herself.

When the plane touched down in Atlanta after less than an hour in the air, the peanuts Mae Lee had eaten had turned her stomach into a full-service gas pump. Once inside the airport, she made a dash for the rest rooms. She'd barely gotten her girdle down and was preparing to sit down when the toilet flushed. She jumped with a start.

She timidly turned around—and again the toilet flushed—swoosh.

Mae Lee pointed a shaking finger at the toilet. "There you up and go again with your little fast self."

Afterward when she attempted to wash her hands she couldn't find a way to turn the water faucet on. "This is crazy," she groaned aloud.

"Did you say something, hon?" It was the woman who sat on the same row with her on the plane. She was leaning toward the mirror, spreading on layers of bright red lipstick.

"Oh, it's you again," Mae Lee brightened. "I'm trying to get water. How do you turn this thing on?"

168

"Just hold your hands under the faucet."

The water gushed out. "Well, I'll be," Mae Lee said. Now she's probably wondering how dumb can I be, she thought.

Mae Lee couldn't believe the prices on the dinner menu at the hotel. The chicken must have gold in it to cost so much, she thought.

She looked up at the young black waiter pouring her iced tea. "Who are your people? Is your mama living?" she asked.

Taken by surprise, the young man grinned and said only, "Yes, ma'am."

Later Mae Lee accepted another serving of tea from the waiter and slowly nibbled on her dinner. The serving was so small she could have finished it in a few bites. By eating slowly she hoped to feel at least a little bit full. At least the iced tea would help. She would drink them dry; it was the only way she could handle having paid so much for it.

She examined a thinly sliced strawberry fanned out beside her slice of cheesecake, trying to envision the edge of a knife sharp enough to cut slices so thin and even. She didn't want to leave it on her plate, but she had done so because she'd glanced at the ladies at the table next to her, and even though they'd finished eating, half of all that high-priced food was still left on their plates. So she'd cut her strawberry into even smaller pieces and scattered it around her empty plate. Leaving that piece of good fruit to be thrown away, however, had fretted her.

Left along with the strawberries was a small, bite-size piece of cheesecake. A waiter reached for her plate. "Hold on there, young man," she bellowed out. "There is still something to eat on my plate." The waiter apologized and backed away.

Mae Lee's children had given her extra money so that she could enjoy the luxury of having breakfast delivered to her room. She checked the items off for her first breakfast on her menu, then changed her mind. She didn't want the cleaning maid to come into her room before she had a chance to tidy it up a bit, much less some stranger knocking on her door with a breakfast tray. So she dressed and went down to the dining room.

"You are such a pretty little thing," she said to the young woman at the front desk. "You look like my daughters. They put me up here to go see the Braves play. How do I find a taxi to get over there?"

The woman pointed to a man at a desk. "The concierge will help you. God bless," she smiled.

The man at the desk, who wore a perfectly pressed dark suit and white shirt, moved and spoke with the airs of a funeral director. His skin was so pale it seemed the sun held something against it and had refused to shine upon it. He pulled his lips into a fake smile, taut lips stretched and tacked into the corners of his mouth.

Mae Lee was too anxious to get to the Braves game to sit down and wait. She didn't need the doorman to tell her taxis were there. She could see them, all lined up right outside the lobby door.

Outside a well-dressed, gray-haired woman waited for somebody.

"I like your beads," Mae Lee said.

The woman smiled. "My granddaughter made them. She's only twelve, but can you believe she's already set up her own little mail order company. My husband is her business manager." She grinned mischievously. "He's a retired architect and it's great getting him out of the house a few days a week. If you give me your address I'll mail you a string of those beads."

Mae Lee drew in a deep breath and eyed the pretty beads. "How much is all this going to cost me?" she asked.

The woman threw her head back and laughed. A lot of metal showed. "Oh, it'll be a little gift from me. Anything to give them an order to fill." A handsome, white-haired man headed toward them. The woman dropped her voice. "Believe me, they don't cost that much to make."

Mae Lee wrote her name and address on a small piece of paper. She looked at the woman. "Do you have daughters?"

"No, four sons."

Mae Lee thanked the woman and got into one of the waiting cabs. She waved good-bye as the cab pulled away from the hotel. Mae Lee peered through the taxicab window. In a run-down section of town, a stalled car brought traffic to a standstill on the narrow one-way street. Even with houses, the people seemed to live on the streets. On a front porch in plain view of passersby a hungry child with scads of pink bows on its head pulled away on the uncovered breast of a sleeping woman. A group of small children huddled close by, some possibly waiting their turn. The woman, seated on a worn velvet sofa, wore a jeans skirt and a soiled pink slip, but her hair was fashionably cut and curled. Her brown skin, perfect nose, and cheekbones were flawless. Her beautiful face offered, even in sleep, a portrait of hopelessness and despair. Mae Lee studied the old tattered sofa. It made her think about her overstuffed chair that was getting pretty frayed. She needed to have it reupholstered, or get a new one someday.

"The homeless are everywhere," Mae Lee said to the driver. "I don't know why I always seemed to think it was only in the North."

The driver turned his radio down. "It's a problem in all big cities."

On a doorstep a young girl perched, raking long bright red nails that looked like falcon claws through her long hair. It pulled up a mental image of what Mae Lee had always imagined was the way the mad, dethroned King Nebuchadnezzar might have clawed through his seven-year growth of uncut, snarled, and matted hair.

A young man with beady, racing eyes knocked on the cab window. "Can you let me have fifty cents?" he begged.

The cab driver looked at Mae Lee through his rearview mirror and shook his head, no. Mae Lee handed the young beggar a dollar bill.

In a parked car, a man openly exposed himself. She didn't think people did that anymore. It made her sick to her stomach, but she looked anyway.

Finally the traffic started to move. As they drove on, Mae Lee's eyes searched the streets and park benches. She shook her head, not in disgust, but out of pity. They moved onto the throughway, and Mae Lee read the road signs that pointed to the airport. The cab driver rounded a curve and there on the left was the Braves' stadium. Mae Lee tilted her head for a better view.

"It's really big," Mae Lee said, peering out the window at the stadium. "How much is my fare?"

The cab driver pointed to the meter. "Nine dollars and eighty-five cents," he said.

Mae Lee paid the exact amount, counting out the change to the nickel. She leaned forward to the front seat and handed the driver the money. He took it, hesitated, and cleared his throat. Mae Lee realized she'd forgotten his tip. Taylor had told her to be generous with cab drivers, because their tips were their wages. She gave him two dollars.

She moved with the surging noisy crowd to the inside of the stadium and stood gaping at the size of it. Except on television, she'd never seen anything like it. She stopped dead in her tracks with a tight hold on her ticket stub. She shook her head. "How in the Lord's name will I ever find where I'm supposed to park my body?"

A passerby brushed against her. "Mind your manners, young fellow," she called out. She reached to hold on to her hat. From what she could see, she was the only person there wearing a hat.

When she finally found her seat, she was exhausted. But her tiredness left when the game started.

"Come on, come on," she called out to the leadoff batter for the Braves. "You can do it, you can do it. Put a little more power to it!"

"Aw, damn," she screamed later when a Braves outfielder let a fly ball get right through his glove. Heads turned, and she felt uncomfortable. She had been around her son, Taylor, too long. But she stiffened her back and bristled, "Well, the dummy dropped it, didn't he?"

The Braves scored, and were back in her favor. "Go on, go on," she shouted. "All the way to the World Series, on to the World Series, boys!" she shouted.

The Braves won the baseball game and Mae Lee felt sure that she'd helped them win it.

On the plane trip home she was more relaxed. When she boarded the U.S. Air flight there was a pretty woman standing in the cockpit doorway. She smiled at Mae Lee.

Mae Lee paused. "Are you going to help fly this big thing?"

The woman nodded, "Yes, I've been doing it for fifteen years."

"I'm proud of you honey, real proud!"

She leaned back in her seat. The takeoff was smooth. She was glad to be heading home. There had been too many days that all seemed like Sunday.

Taylor, Bettina, and their children and Ellabelle were waiting for her when she got off the plane. The girls held a big cardboard sign, "WELCOME HOME MAE LEE." She smothered her two granddaughters, Tina and Lena, with hugs, kisses, and gifts. "When did you start to call your grandma by her first name?" she teased. She kissed them good-bye and left to go home with Ellabelle.

Mae Lee had offered no explanation for the grease stains on the presents and postcards she'd brought back. She could not bring herself to tell what being so cheap had wrought.

Jelly and butter had oozed from the breakfast croissants and muffins she'd wrapped in Kleenex and stashed in the bag to eat for her lunch. If they didn't want them, they could give them back.

Ellabelle didn't wait until they reached home to tell Mae Lee the sad news that Church Granger had died. "He was on a fishing trip and had a heart attack." Ellabelle snapped her fingers. "Just like that he was gone. Dead, at the age of sixty-three. I saved the death notice from the newspaper for you."

Mae Lee remembered the day she bought the land from Church Granger, but most importantly, the time Taylor was sick. She would never forget his kindness. "I'm so sorry," she said. "Church Granger was a fine man." She wondered whether Liddie came back for the funeral.

She closed her eyes and grew silent. She was shaken and saddened by the news.

: 15 :

Several weeks later Mae Lee was in bed at 9:00 p.m. when her phone rang. It was Ellabelle.

"I don't know whether you've got your TV on, but there's a tornado warning for Tally County—up until 10:00 p.m."

Mae Lee hadn't heard. She turned her bedside lamp on. "I wasn't feeling too well this evening, so I went to bed early. I'm glad you were watching," she said.

"I wasn't," Ellabelle answered. "I was so tired this evening I had put my weary bones in bed when Clairene called with the news about the tornado. She said she'd already taken her nightgown off and put on an old pair of her husband's pants to sleep in, just in case she'd have to rush out in the storm. You never know what will happen. You get up and slip on a pair of panties, Mae Lee. That's what I'm fixing to do. I've laid out a brand spanking new pair. In case that tornado strikes, I'm not gonna be stuck up in some tree hanging out with my bare bottom showing."

176

Outside the house there was a sharp flash of lightning followed by a blast of thunder. "Oh, Lord," Mae Lee said. "Bye, bye!" She hung up the telephone. She jumped out of bed, grabbed up some blankets, and ran into the kitchen. She draped them over the curtain rods so they would cover the kitchen windows, pushed the table into a corner, and brought in her rocking chair.

Someone had said that if a tornado came, the proper thing to do was to get under a stairwell. She didn't have one. If she had to, she would dive under the heavy oak table. With her robe pulled tightly around her, she huddled in the rocker.

Mae Lee worried whether Lou Esther and Warren had been warned. She wanted to call them, but was afraid to talk on the telephone during a storm. At least they had something good to eat. Only the afternoon before Mae Lee hand-carried over a big basket of fried chicken, homemade hot biscuits, and vegetable soup. Warren was now retired, and his health was starting to fail.

Mae Lee thought of how, years earlier, Church Granger had driven to outlying farmhouses to warn the families without telephones of an approaching hurricane. For a fleeting second, she wondered if he knew about the tornado watch, but then remembered that the poor soul did not need to be called.

The storm was raging all about the house, and there she was, alone in her kitchen, rocking and thinking, her eyes tightly closed yet still seeing the brilliant flashes of lightning. Although the storm was frightening, Mae Lee's thoughts were even more so. She'd been roused from a troubled sleep. Maybe she'd heard the whirling wind outside, but she had been dreaming about some story she'd read in the paper. Now she couldn't get the story out of her mind. Things she read about total strangers rarely affected her so much. But this story, about a young dancer's death, had worried her. At the young age of twenty-one, the dancer's life was cut short because of AIDS.

Mae Lee had studied the dancer's picture. The dancer was flying through the air. She'd thought of him as a little air-dancer. And now the picture of the air-dancer was heaping anxiety and grief upon her. The image of her grandson's face the first time she saw the fool earring in his ear flashed before her.

She couldn't remember if the air-dancer had an earring in his ear. Though the newspaper was right there in the kitchen, she made no effort to look. If the air-dancer had worn an earring, she didn't want to know. The earring business bothered her.

In the face of an impending tornado, Mae Lee forced herself to confront truth. Was she more worried about Mae Lee Barnes's image than her grandson, more concerned over what people might think of her because of her grandson's earring?

It was too much. Mae Lee started crying. She thought of the dates in the newspaper chronicling the life of the young man—his birth, his great successes, his tragic death. And now she cried for him, the little twenty-one-year-old dancer.

Yet it was more even than the earring in her grandson's left ear that she was worried about. When she allowed herself to really be honest with herself, she worried about her own mind. Sometimes she would be telling someone something very important, and then right in the middle she'd forget the point she intended to make. And try though she might, she just couldn't remember.

The lightning and thunder seemed to have died down for a while. It was quiet and calm now. She turned on the kitchen light. Before the storm started up again, she needed to know where her money was so she could get it in case she had to get out of the house in a hurry. She moved the money bag from her umbrella stand, placed it in the bottom of her rice canister, and covered it over with rice.

It was good she still remembered where the money was. The other day she'd forgotten where she'd hidden it and spent the better portion of the day looking before she found it. Was she losing her mind?

Mae Lee picked up an advertisement for a new local nursing home. She'd saved it to give to Clairene. Clairene was going to have to put her mother-in-law into a home. The women at the hospital had talked about how blessed they were. They believed it would take some doing to force their children to come down to putting them into a home.

She thought of Ellabelle's sister tucked away in a nursing home. Her children had talked the poor old soul into putting her house in their names, then they seemed to sit back and wait for her to break some bone so they could put her away. But as she and Ellabelle had agreed, those children all lived in the North. So often when people moved to the North, they changed their ways, their thinking, and they didn't rightly realize what they were doing. If those children had stayed in South Carolina, they wouldn't have done such a thing.

The very thought of the North made Mae Lee sit upright

in her rocking chair. Three of her children lived in the North and the other two, although nearby, still lived in North Carolina. She hoped the word "north" hadn't messed up that part of the South.

Mae Lee felt uneasy. She had been feeling poorly all day. She looked at the nursing home advertisement again, and thought of her friend Claude Madison. The poor thing broke his leg, and while it was true that maybe his frail daughter in the North couldn't take care of him, he had let her talk him into going into a nursing home until he was better. After all, he could have stayed on with his sister, who was old but spry and in good health.

At first when she'd visited him in the nursing home, he was happily looking forward to his leg healing and coming back home. In time his broken leg healed, but by then his spirit was broken. The last time she visited him, he made no mention of coming home. He didn't mention anything, just sat there, staring at the blank walls. Claude Madison never came home.

She didn't know what being in a nursing home did to a person's mind when they were forced to stay there even when they were well. She decided she'd better be careful and not break any bones.

Mae Lee and the ladies down at the hospital had often talked about nursing homes and had said that children generally didn't mean any harm when they rushed their aged parents off to nursing homes. So often they just weren't mature enough to fully understand, that was all. She felt sure that her children would never put her away.

Mae Lee could sense a quiet fear—that uncertain kind of

fear that starts to creep in on people when they are alone in the night and already scared to death. And now there it was, fear closing in on her like wind-pushed rain clouds. She grabbed up a small brown paper bag and began writing. When she finished, she safety-pinned it to the nursing home ad.

My children,

My old right arm is aching me again so I hope you can read this chicken-scratching. It's not hurting too bad though, so don't you worry. The doctor said it is just arthritis. Maybe someday one of you children might lay something like this newspaper ad out for me to see. Please never tell me it's time to go into one of these places. Children, don't ever put me in no place like that. I don't care how they smile and carry on in those pictures. They are not happy. How could they be? Nobody can be happy away from their own home. How could I be happy away from here? I took care of you when you were weedie bitty babies. Now it's your turn. I'm your baby now. Take care of me.

Mama

P.S. I shouldn't be too much trouble. There is only one of me and I pray there will still be five of you. But if you all ever feel it's too much, children, you can always put me up for adoption.

As quickly as the storm had seemed to end, now it started again—the lightning flashed, the thunder roared, and racing, churning winds rocked the new house.

The roar of the wind was frightening. Something crashed

against the house. The thunder was deafening. The back screen door, blown loose by the ripping winds, flapped back and forth. Pieces of limbs torn from the trees crashed against the roof with such force she thought for sure some of them would come through.

The mournful sound of the wind was almost human. The image of her handsome young grandson's face flashed before Mae Lee's eyes as plainly as the lightning. "On second thought," she whispered to herself, "maybe I remember more than I need to." The memories of the summers her grandson had spent with her were sharp and clear. Sweet memories now soured by the thought of that earring. It didn't matter what some might say. For her, it wasn't natural for a boy to want to wear an earring in his ear. But then, maybe she was partly to blame. She'd bought a little boy a little girl's nursing kit.

Now, sitting alone in the kitchen, alternately dark and light by the flashing lightning, she was troubled that maybe she shouldn't have bought the little nurse's kit. Her mama had always told her never to allow her son, Taylor, to play with his sisters' girl toys and baby dolls.

Mae Lee tried to swallow the lump that sadness had welled up in her throat, but the attempt made it worse. Tears burned her eyes. She found it difficult to breathe. The combination of sadness and fear was choking. She knew that the eerie sounds outside belonged to a windstorm that could suck its fury into a long funnel-shaped cloud extending toward the ground, and decide what was to be spared or destroyed.

She prayed silently that her grandson wouldn't be somewhere mixed up with the wrong crowd, speeding down highways with a crowd of youngsters with little hickory-nut–sized heads rising just above steering wheels. She prayed her grandson's mama wouldn't allow him to have his full head of hair cut so that in spite of being a husky healthy young man he would still look like a little midget in a car. She hated little pointed-looking heads.

Mae Lee thought of all the time she had spent on her grandson's head, shaping and smoothing, turning the sleeping baby so he'd have a round pretty head. She hated to see some crazy, pointed haircut come along and destroy it all. It seemed to her that if a young boy wanted his head to look like he was wearing a dunce cap, he could go and buy one.

Sitting in the dark, riding out the storm alone, she blamed herself for having read the newspaper article about the death of the ballet dancer in the first place. Maybe it was good to know about things going on in the world, to keep up with the news and all, but so often knowing brought pain. Sometimes she kind of wished that she was more like her distant cousin Mamie. The woman couldn't read or write. She still didn't believe that man walked on the moon, yet she was happy as a lark, and oh, could she sing.

She couldn't help thinking that sometimes they even put too much in the newspapers. In one article she'd read that left-handed people had a shorter life span. Her grandson Tread was left-handed.

She reached for the glass of water she'd placed on the table. A glass of water and a plate of Sweet Sour Cream Roll-Ups. The tornado might take her away, she thought, but she sure didn't plan to go thirsty or hungry.

She picked up her glass of water with her left hand. She too was left-handed. Her mama had also been left-handed. Her grandson had inherited his grandmother's genes. He couldn't help being a lefty. Maybe he couldn't help wanting to wear an earring in his left ear.

Mae Lee shivered, pulled a cotton blanket about her shoulders, gathered the stones she was all set to cast, and mentally buried them. "I'm driving myself crazy," she said aloud. "Crazy over nothing."

Suddenly her worries and anxious concerns over what people would think, including her own suspicions, paled away. Maybe Ellabelle had been right about the earring thing. Maybe, like Dallace said, it was after all in Tread's left ear.

She thought of her young grandson's eyes that day, eyes that begged for her acceptance. She'd read that, but had withheld her acceptance. Now, in the face of a storm that might sweep her away, she found it in her heart to forgive. "Grandmama forgives," she cried out repeatedly. Her cries were muffled by the whistling winds and drowned out by the thunder. Her grandchild did not have to be present for her to feel fulfilled.

"I'm Tread Wallace's grandma." She smiled finally. "He is my firstborn grandson, and that's all that really matters. For now, that's enough."

The next morning the sun streamed in on Mae Lee, sound asleep in her rocking chair. It crept across her body like a cat stalking a small bird. She awoke refreshed. She had slept out both a tornado and her troubles too.

Part : V

: 16 :

During the last week in November 1989, only a month away from the date Hooker Jones had set to kill hogs and make all that tasty fresh sausage and liver pudding, Mae Lee's doctor ordered her to cut all pork out of her diet.

As she eyed the meats in the Be-Lo grocery store she thought of what Dr. Bell had said: "No pork, Mae Lee." For a long time she studied the meats. Moving along the line she finally picked up a package of chicken, but put it back. She was so tired of chicken. The cuts of beef looked good, but she passed them by.

Mae Lee felt sad. For years she had not been able to afford the meats and desserts she loved. Now she could afford them, only she couldn't have them, because they caused high blood pressure and cholesterol.

She glanced over at the pork meat again. Her heart heavy, she looked at the things in her shopping cart. A little piece of pork would set her dinner off. Like a crook about to shoplift something, she quickly glanced about to see whether the coast was clear, then started sorting through the country-style pork ribs.

"Mae Lee Barnes?" a soft voice behind her called out.

Mae Lee jumped. The package of pork fell to the floor. For a brief moment Mae Lee stared at the white woman standing before her, the large blue eyes and thin pale hair, the face filled with wrinkles. "Miz Granger? Liddie Granger?" she questioned. "Is that you?"

Liddie Granger nervously twisted a wedding ring around her slender fingers. Blue veins bulged in her white hands. Her hands looked really old. Finally, she smiled. "Yes, Mae Lee, it's me. What's left of me. I didn't realize I'd changed that much."

"Changed? Huh, you haven't changed a speck. You look as good now as you did when I first met you. And that's saying something. You were the prettiest girl in Rising Ridge." And that's the Lord's truth on that, Mae Lee thought to herself, but oh, Lord, don't strike me speechless for the bald-faced lie before that.

Mae Lee picked up her meat. "No, I'm not supposed to eat it but I do," she explained, laughing. "Dr. Bell would have a fit if he saw me loading this pork meat into my shopping cart."

Mae Lee grew serious, her voice was tinged with sadness. "I'm sorry about the death of Church. You have my deepest sympathy."

Liddie Granger smiled. It helped in a small way to ease the pained sadness in her face. "Thank you, Mae Lee." There was a faraway look in Liddie Granger's eyes. "My son was alone in the house after his father died, so I decided to come back to be here for him. But, oh, Mae Lee, the house is so lonely now. You should come and visit me when you come out to your old home place. I always think of you when I look towards the place where your old house used to stand. I used to envy you so. You seemed so free-spirited and happy. Way back then, you got a divorce and went on with your life," she said.

Mae Lee laughed. "Those days weren't so very easy for me," she said. She was puzzled over what Liddie had said about her divorce. She knew Liddie could have gotten a divorce if she'd wanted to. It surprised her to know that she'd apparently thought about it, even back then. It all serves to teach me a lesson or two, Mae Lee thought. Never envy someone like I envied Liddie Granger unless you know what you're envious of. They'd seemed so happy. Church loved his children. But Liddie was not his daughter, she was his wife.

Liddie Granger looked at Mae Lee. "I've made a lot of mistakes over the years." There were tears in her eyes.

Oh, no, Mae Lee thought when she saw Liddie's eyes had misted over, don't allow yourself to get all tore up right here in the store. Everybody will see you, and you know how quick people in this town are to talk. I can't begin to put in my mind what some folks would make out of seeing you crying in front of the liver mush and fatback meat counter. "Bet she's run through all that money Church Granger left her" would be the first thing they'd say. Women and some men tend to get all teary-eyed and religious when their family fortune is gone, or as Nellie Grace would say, just before election campaigns when they or their husbands are running for some political office. She shook her head.

Liddie Granger started to ask Mae Lee about her children, and to tell about her own children almost at the same time, but she rambled, getting a little confused along the way. There she was, getting confused, and she was younger than Mae Lee. Not by much, but still younger. Mae Lee listened, her fingers digging into a loaf of Wonder wheat bread in her shopping cart. Her girls had fussed so about the calories in white bread that she'd stopped buying it altogether.

She studied Liddie Granger's face. It had that fragile haunted look that a white woman with that much money shouldn't have. I hope she isn't heading for a nervous breakdown, Mae Lee thought to herself. She watched the frail woman dab at her eyes. Liddie Granger had drawn Mae Lee into a spider's web; she was held captive.

Mae Lee held on to her bread loaf with both hands. She glanced about the busy shoppers inside the store and hoped that Liddie Granger, on the verge of tears, wouldn't break down. She half-listened as Liddie chattered on and on about earlier days on the farm; Mae Lee could only think that Liddie Granger had no business being that disturbed and sad. Mae Lee had known her mama and daddy before they passed on. Liddie was a very rich woman, was rich even before she married Church and then became richer. There shouldn't have been any reason she should have been so unhappy, unless— well, maybe there had been something awful in her life that nobody knew about.

Mae Lee tried to sort out her thoughts, but it was like picking your way through a swamp with quicksand suck holes. You just don't know what goes on behind closed doors or what reasons somebody might have for wanting a divorce, she decided.

Liddie seemed to pull herself together. She picked up a small package of pork chops. Her sadness was still there though. "I wish so much that things had been different between Church and me. He was a good man in so many ways. Oh, God, I miss him so."

Mae Lee breathed a sigh of relief. She didn't want her memory of Church Granger tainted.

Liddie looked at Mae Lee's loaf of bread and laughed. The loaf looked like a wrung-out heavy towel. "I heard that you're one of the hospital volunteers, Mae Lee," Liddie said. "You probably don't have a lot of free time, but please come out to see me sometimes when you get a chance."

"And you do the same," Mae Lee urged. "Come by and see me anytime."

They parted ways. At the end of the aisle, the two women turned and waved a second good-bye. Liddie disappeared behind a mountain of paper towels on sale, and Mae Lee stood staring after her. Poor Liddie, she thought. She's sleeping under the same quilt of guilt with thousands of other women. She still has husband trouble even after the man is in his grave. Mae Lee shook her head. And to think that all these years she had thought the pot of gold at the end of the rainbow was in Liddie Granger's front yard.

She drew a long, heavy sigh. The wild plums are always sweeter on someone else's land, she thought.

: 17 :

More than two years had gone by since Mae Lee first began her volunteer work at the hospital. It was spring and she welcomed the warm days.

The ladies in the hospital volunteer group had a program of going on a tour twice each year. They chartered a bus and spent two nights away. The first several times when Mae Lee was asked whether she wanted to go she declined. But then she decided to go along the next time just to see what it was like. The tour this spring was to be along the Carolina and Georgia coast, including Charleston and Savannah, to see the old homes and plantations.

At exactly seven o'clock in the morning, ten minutes before the tour bus was scheduled to leave, Mae Lee climbed aboard and picked out her seat, in the front near the driver. She held her head high. On the outside she was just another passenger. Inside she was Rosa Parks, years earlier down in Alabama. It was a role she never tired of playing.

She watched the passengers board the bus. Most of her fellow hospital volunteers were not really well-to-do women, she thought, but they had the money to go when and where they wanted.

The bus driver, a handsome, clean-shaven young black man, helped the last passenger get her small bag inside the bus. "I work with them two or three days a week," she explained to the driver after he took his seat at the wheel. She leaned forward so the others couldn't hear her over the engine. "I do volunteer work at a hospital. I've been in their homes, and they've been in mine. But the thing this time is, I've never been around them in this capacity before. Know what I mean?"

"I catch your drift," the bus driver said.

The spring was perfect for a bus tour in the Low Country of South Carolina. When the bus reached Charleston, the azaleas were in full bloom and the magnolia tree buds were swelling. The group checked into a Hampton Inn. Mae Lee thought the room rate that the others considered so reasonable was quite costly. They were only going to sleep there. Shortly after they checked in, they boarded the bus again and were off traveling across the Cooper River to view the handsome mansions and gardens and to lunch at one of the many restaurants offering the fresh daily catches brought in by the fishing fleets.

The next morning Mae Lee was up early, anxiously awaiting the trip across the Ashley River to Savannah, Georgia. At least she knew one thing about Savannah. It was not far from there that Eli Whitney invented the cotton gin, a mechanized method of ginning seed from cotton, which was why slaves became so valuable to their owners.

Again Mae Lee was drawn to the graveyards, and the old restored plantation homes. Just walking the grounds of a home outside Savannah that once had teemed with slave servants evoked an indescribable feeling of kinship within her. The thought that maybe her ancestors had walked on the very same soil was overwhelming. With cold chills surging through her body, she walked, her eyes searching for anything that might offer a trace of her roots. She didn't have to be on the shores of the Atlantic to do that.

She knew what she was looking for, what she hoped to find. For as long as she could remember, she had heard the story that went back to her great-grandfather, a man called Samwasi, a slave who left only a number and a drawing as the clue for his descendants to trace their heritage. Her daddy, Sam, had been named after him. His drawing showed, Mae Lee had been told, the number four and a scythe, perfectly drawn to scale, unmistakably clear. Time and time again, the story went, the slave had drawn this image in the loose dirt at his feet. "He couldn't read or write," her daddy had told her. "This is all we know about where our people might be buried."

In a seemingly forsaken corner at the edge of the woods in one old cemetery, the tour guide pointed out the graves of slaves. After the group moved on, Mae Lee had stood so long staring at the graves that Bethel Petty returned to see if she was all right.

The tour guide didn't explain the meaning behind the rusting chain links scattered about on a few graves, Mae Lee pointed this out to Bethel Petty. The three links joined together meant that the dead slave was born into slavery, worked and

194

lived as a slave, and died as a slave, Mae Lee explained. She pointed to the scattered links of a broken chain, breathed a sigh of relief, and said softly, "The broken chain shows that this slave had gained her freedom."

Mae Lee had not been prepared for Bethel Petty's reaction when she told her that given time, she would no doubt find the number four and a scythe drawn by her great-grandfather somewhere, possibly in or near some graveyard. "A four and a scythe?" Bethel Petty's eyes narrowed, then opened wide. Her voice was edged with excitement. "Oh, Mae Lee," the words rushed from her, "it must be Forsyth, Georgia. Forsyth County, Georgia!"

"I never heard of that place," Mae Lee said.

"It's the county in *Gone with the Wind*. It's right outside of Atlanta."

Maybe Bethel Petty was right, Mae Lee thought. If she went looking she might be able to find the place. But there must be hundreds of graveyards outside a big city like Atlanta. Besides, slaves weren't given granite tombstones when they died; the most they could expect would be wooden planks with their names on them, which would have long since disappeared. Still—

"Someday I'd like to go looking," she said.

"Oh, Mae Lee, wouldn't it be exciting if you could find something?" Bethel Petty declared. "I'd love to go with you to look for it!" Her eyes beamed with the excitement of a person setting out on a treasure hunt.

Mae Lee turned for a final look. Aside from the few graves with the rusty chains, the graves were unmarked and not well tended. But there were the lilies. According to the tour guide they voluntarily surfaced and bloomed each spring.

She wondered what great sacrifices some of the slaves had to make to save enough money to buy their freedom. She thought about how hard they must have worked, and of where they might have hidden their money. Perhaps she shared a common bond in hiding money; she hoped the habit had been passed down, from her great-grandfather Samwasi. The very idea made her feel her money was securely hidden.

Mae Lee followed along on the tour, hanging on to the tour guide's every word, never showing any signs of the pain that often brought tears to her eyes behind her sunglasses. It was the thought of the mistreatment, the forced labor, and the breakup of families that hurt most.

She remembered the torn quilt that had been handed down for generations in her daddy's family. She felt satisfaction because the torn quilt was where it should be, with her baby girl, Amberlee. Her mama, Vergie, had given her the quilt when she was fifteen. Amberlee had not known that, yet when she turned fifteen she'd begged her for the quilt. Since none of the others had asked for it, Mae Lee decided it was meant to be hers.

She had explained the strings attached. The quilt must always be kept in the family. It represented families that had been stitched together by women of many generations. If or when the quilt was torn, according to legend, it was because it needed to open up to make room for a piece of another family member's garment. A custom passed down from the days of slavery, it all started with a slave woman's prayer that perhaps through a family patchwork quilt the memory of a piece of a garment might serve as a clue to identify and reunite a family broken apart and children sold off at an early age. It had been a mother's way of stitching a family together. It was the thread of the family heritage that bound them together.

Once her little Amberlee had clipped a picture of a black family from a magazine and put it in her little white cardboard shoebox. Mae Lee could never forget the faces of the family in the picture. The memory was like a movie that played over and over in her mind, a smiling father, mother, and children. So it shouldn't have surprised her when she discovered the picture of an elderly man, unknown to her, in her daughter's apartment. But it did hurt somewhat to learn that Amberlee had been passing him off as her paternal grandfather.

"Who is this paternal grandfather of yours, as you call him?" Mae Lee had asked.

"I don't know who the man is, Mama. I bought the portrait at an auction."

Mae Lee had studied the equally pained look in her daughter's face. "And what kind of grandfather is that?"

Her daughter didn't turn to face her. "It means, Mama, it means," she stammered, "I'm pretending that he is my daddy's daddy."

Mae Lee moved closer to the elegantly framed oval picture. "So mamas don't count anymore." She drew a deep breath, then said softly, "He is a handsome grandfather. Very handsome indeed."

"Mama," her daughter pleaded, "you do count. You always will. It's just that there is a lot of interest right now in family history. Some of my friends can trace their roots so far back, it's, well, a little embarrassing for me to be hardly able to go back to my own father on his side of the family. So I just gave this picture a name and hung it up."

Yes, Mae Lee reassured herself, it was right that the torn family quilt should end up with Amberlee.

The next two days were very much like the first two. From mansion to mansion, the historical accounts went on and on. But as for the slaves, when there was some rare recorded recognition of their contribution, it had only been for some honor bestowed for serving the master who owned them faithfully and with fidelity until death.

The quarters and cemeteries held her spellbound. Her eyes were always searching, poring over every mark or notch, looking for something, perhaps a few stones piled or shaped into some pattern, that might fit into her mind's puzzle and offer some fragile link in her family's broken and scattered chain.

Mae Lee fingered her brochures and looked upon the places they described. Could this be the house, she wondered, where her foreparent had loudly whistled his way from the kitchen through the breezeway while carrying food to the master's table? Her foreparent, according to stories passed down through generations, who had mastered the art of holding snippets of food under his tongue and in his cheeks and whistling loudly at the same time?

So Mae Lee continued her quiet search.

On the way home Mae Lee gazed at the trees alongside the interstate. They were lovely in the spring, white dogwood trees weaving a pattern into the lush green trees like white lace trimming on a dark green dress. Growing in between here and there was the beautiful bright fuchsia-flowered redbud tree, called the Judas tree. The tree grew weak and crooked. After all, she thought, it represented a crooked man, Judas.

"I bet if I could get this tree home, growing up in my backyard would straighten it out. If you pull this bus over, I'll hop out and jerk up a few offshoots from those pretty trees," she hinted hopefully to the driver.

"Probably wouldn't live."

"Oh, it would live all right. I've got a green thumb."

The bus driver smiled, but did not break his speed.

Less than a month after Mae Lee returned from what she swore would be the last bus tour she'd ever take just before the spring planting season, her farming plans fell apart. She was worrying over a flat tire on her wheelbarrow when she learned that Hooker Jones had suffered a stroke. His farming days were over. The doctors didn't expect a full recovery.

Mae Lee's efforts to find someone to take over the farmwork were fruitless. For the first time in well over sixty years the land would not be cultivated. It was good farmland. The soil had been kept fertile through careful crop rotation. Mae Lee had learned that from her daddy. Even so, there were no takers for the job. People throughout the South were leaving the farming life.

Mae Lee's son, Taylor, also tried to find someone to lease the land, without success. "You've got to face it, Mama, farming is too much of a losing gamble these days," Taylor said.

Mae Lee grew quiet. "The farm brought in real good money last year," she finally said.

"I know, but what about the years before, Mama? You'd do better on the money end to rent out granddaddy's house until some offer comes along from someone who wants to buy or lease the land," Taylor said.

Mae Lee eyed her son. "What about Hooker and his wife?"

"Mama, they can't afford to pay the kind of rent that house will bring."

"They can afford to pay what I'm going to charge them, because it's going to be whatever they can give." Mae Lee stared at her son in disbelief. "Taylor, you weren't too young to remember all those years they helped pull me through. Hooker and Maycie Jones would finish gathering their crops and then help me with mine. And you think they would accept pay? Not a penny. Why? Because I was a woman with five children to raise. One doesn't forget people like that, son, one doesn't forget."

Taylor thought for a moment, then turned to face his mama. "I'm ashamed of myself, Mama," he said. "So ashamed." He kissed his mama and left.

Later, in her kitchen, Mae Lee spooned soup from a big pot into a small bowl. Sometimes she couldn't remember if she'd added salt or not. She took a taste and made a face. She added a pinch of salt and pepper to the soup and put a pan of biscuits in the oven to bake. She removed a few more pieces of baked chicken legs and breasts off the piled-up platters she was taking to Warren and the Joneses, and rolled out another pan of biscuits, enough for Ellabelle if she cared to eat, and Ellabelle would.

The singing voice of Elvis Presley on the radio made her step back in time. She remembered some remark he'd made about her people. They were called "colored people" then. And as she'd done then and from the day since she'd heard about it, she would refuse even to listen to him sing if she could do anything about it. She reached out to turn off her radio. Then she stopped. Elvis Presley was dead. Died in disgrace, when he was still a young man. And she was alive. The radio stayed on.

"Age sure has a way of causing you to turn around," she said aloud. "It softens you. When you are young you find it so easy to decide whether you think a person is good or bad. When you are old you think of what made them good or bad and take that into account."

Ellabelle helped load the food into her car. After they brought the Joneses their food basket, Mae Lee asked Ellabelle to stop her car near her old house. Ellabelle decided to wait in the car when Mae Lee said she wanted to walk to her cousin's house.

She wanted to walk the old small wagon road along which she'd hurried back and forth so many times. The road was somewhat overgrown, but she wanted to take it anyway. She used a heavy stick to push the bramble and underbrush aside. She paused now and then to listen to the sounds riding the winds. Wind chimes of the morning.

In a small clearing in the woods, the frame of an abandoned and rusting car peeped from under clusters of overgrowth. Its still shiny grill and exposed headlights, adorned with blooming wildflowers and the green flowers on the creeping poison ivy, shone forth like mirrors.

Mae Lee placed her food basket on a tree stump and studied the huge oak tree beside the old car, and for a few moments it seemed she saw her children playing there, heard their happy playful cries: "Doodle bug, doodle bug, come on out . . . your house is on fire. . . ." She could almost hear the sound of her hoe making its musical clinking sounds when she struck small rocks on her cotton row. She could smell the freshly plowed ground, feel the cool soil underneath her bare feet in the freshly plowed furrows. She could hear the gee, haw commands her daddy called out to Maude, his faithful old mule. Turn to the right, turn to the left.

Mae Lee lingered for a final look at the old car—a thing of beauty even in its tangled setting. She'd never seen it before. She wondered how long it had been there. Maybe, she thought, the cussing widow from the curious family down the road had caused the car to run off the road one night and end up there. She remembered how the woman used to dig ditches across the dirt road to force cars to slow down so they wouldn't run over her chickens. It was said that after she had a few nips of the "special tea" she made she would dig the ditches herself, single-handed, with her hoe.

Maybe one of the widow's sons, like their daddy before them, had taken too many nips of the "special tea," started driving like they walked, from ditch to ditch, and run off the road. She hadn't seen any of them for quite some time. That was not surprising, though. They had always stayed pretty much to themselves. A few months after their mama died, they put a sign in the front yard: "Need a woman to live here." Worse still, maybe it had been some stranger from far away who had wrecked the car there. The thought of who or what may have been in the car was scary.

Something slithered into the undergrowth around the car, rustling the leaves and vines. Mae Lee picked up her basket and hurried on.

Now she couldn't get her thoughts of her mama out of her mind. It seemed Vergie should have been with her on the old wagon road.

After all her efforts, when she reached her cousin's house there was no one home. She had forgotten to call ahead.

: 18 :

The pleasant spring days had quickly pushed the weeks into summer. Mae Lee couldn't bear to think of her good farm soil growing only weeds and blooming wild morning glories. When farmland like that lies barren, your money dries up, Mae Lee thought to herself.

It worried her that she had spent so much money on a house, by far too big for a woman her age, and she fretted that she'd even pinched off her savings to take the bus tour.

I guess spending time around people with more money than you have can't help but affect your spending habits in some way, she thought.

Now that the weather was warm Mae Lee's front porch was starting to come alive again. Her friend Clairene plunked her tired body down on Mae Lee's front steps. "I'm not staying," she announced. She fished around in a big plastic bag and handed Mae Lee an eight-ounce cottage cheese container. "I'm delivering the 'friendship starter bread' today. It's day number ten," she said tiredly. "I've delivered the other two cups. Now remember to follow the directions exactly. Do not use a metal spoon, do not refrigerate, that's day one . . ."

"I know," Mae Lee interrupted. "Do nothing day two, three and four. Stir with wooden spoon, day—aw, shucks, I have the directions. And Clairene, please don't go flashing that old chain letter again. There is no way you're going to get fifty thousand dollars within sixty days just by sending a dollar here and there to people you don't even know."

After Clairene left, Mae Lee headed for the kitchen with the friendship starter bread. But before she had a chance to put it away, there was a knock on her front door.

When she opened it, the clean, neatly dressed, elderly man who stood there seemed respectable enough. He said his name was Fletcher Owens, and he had heard, he said, that she had a room to spare, and he wondered whether she might be willing to take in a roomer.

"I used to live here in Rising Ridge years ago, but my family moved away when I was fairly young," he explained. "We used to live just beyond Catfish Creek in that old frame house down behind the Boyd's farm."

"Oh," Mae Lee said, "you're Phil Owens's nephew." Although she didn't know scat about Fletcher, she did know his people, at least his daddy's family. The Owenses were a close-knit, well-respected family. Eventually they had all moved away from Rising Ridge, but she'd never heard anybody say a cross word about any one of them. She didn't know where they moved to, and had wondered if they'd sold the land they owned, across the Catfish Creek.

She considered herself a good judge of character. And this man was, to all appearances, in his early seventies at least, while she was in her midsixties. Even so, she had been ready to turn Fletcher Owens away until he offered to pay in advance for a room for a few weeks until he found a permanent place to stay. Mae Lee had never in her lifetime thought of renting out a room. But she thought of the money, and the two bedrooms that were empty of use, and agreed to let him stay.

After installing Fletcher Owens in one of the two vacant bedrooms and getting towels and linens for him, Mae Lee took the four fifty-dollar bills he had given her, got out the cotton bag from behind the flour bin in the kitchen where she had moved it last week, and added the money. She now had $5,240. Now she knew why the palm of her hand had been itching so much that morning. That was always a sign of money. It crossed her mind how it might look to her neighbors if she had a man living in her house, but she quickly dismissed it. He would be a roomer. From the moment Mae Lee had laid eyes on this tall handsome man with his flat stomach, she'd labeled him "kind." Her concerns over how her children would feel about it lingered on, however.

She somehow felt that it seemed right and fitting that she should call him Mr. Fletcher, not Mr. Owens, and so she did. After a few days, when Mae Lee had seen Fletcher Owens leave the house every morning before he had had breakfast, she said, "I'll be glad to fix you a little breakfast when I fix my own." Then she'd only had to say, "Why don't you come in and sit down and watch TV with me this evening," for him to make it a regular habit. Fletcher Owens loved television. Mae Lee found they had much in common. They saw the same side of things and loved the same wrong foods. It was all happening so very fast. She started spending less and less time volunteering at the hospital.

She also began sharing little things about her family with him, as well as sharing things about him with Ellabelle and her children. Fletcher laughed with her when she told him that her son, Taylor, wouldn't allow his wife near the kitchen when she visited. Mae Lee spread out her hand like she was smoothing wrinkled empty space. "Every time I go, it's the same thing. Mama cook this. . . . Mama cook that. I always said, 'I'd like to eat your wife's cooking for a change.'"

Fletcher Owens smiled. "I sure would like to meet your Taylor, he seems like a fine young man," he said.

"He wants to meet you, too. He said he'll probably come over here in a few days."

Fletcher smiled. "I'm glad he wants to meet me."

Mae Lee had been a little anxious about them meeting. When they did, she busied herself with her sewing, but she listened. Taylor wasn't blunt or unkind, but he sure didn't beat around the bush. "My mama tells me you are thinking of getting a house in Rising Ridge, Mr. Owens," he said.

Fletcher leaned back in his chair. He appeared calm and relaxed. "Actually, I'm hoping to renovate our old family house if it's not too far gone." He laughed, but quickly grew serious. "I'm retired now, so I've decided to come back to the land where I was born. But it appears that it's going to be quite a struggle to get a clear deed to the land. It's all heir property that's been tied up for a long time. It's going to take some time to get it all untangled. But I suppose the one thing I do have now is time."

That said, he told Taylor stories about his hunting and fishing days. Mae Lee threaded needles with the different thread colors she needed for her embroidery designs and stuck them into a pincushion. She thought of her husband, Taylor's father, how nice it would have been if he had been a man like Fletcher Owens. Taylor had deserved a good daddy. A son needs a daddy.

Later, when Taylor and his mama were alone, Taylor told her that he thought Fletcher Owens seemed very levelheaded and honest. Mae Lee smiled. "I kind of think so too, son. Now you can call your sisters and tell them what you think of your mama's new roomer. And don't raise your eyebrows as if you are surprised, Taylor. You know your sisters asked you to find out what kind of man Mama's new roomer is." Taylor grinned and dropped his head.

It was strange, but she found herself freely telling Fletcher Owens little things that had always embarrassed her. She told him of the day she found out why her daughter had been ashamed of her. She had taken Annie Ruth's lunch to school. The little girl had forgotten it.

She realized later that she had worn one of her faded, loose-fitting, homemade, everyday cotton dresses with white ankle socks and, without thinking, had put on her Sunday dress-up blue straw hat, the one with the red cherries. Little Annie Ruth had kept her head down, barely glancing up at her. "Where are your manners, honey?" she asked. "Aren't you going to tell your little classmates that this is your mama?" Of course she knew them all and they all knew her. Her little Annie Ruth didn't raise her eyes. "This is my mama," she mumbled, grabbed her lunch and ran away.

"You know something, Mr. Fletcher," she said, "when I later noticed my wide body in the mirror in a loose, homemade, cotton dress two sizes too large, I understood why my child had been ashamed. I laughed until I cried." And she and Fletcher Owens laughed some more.

She did wish she hadn't told him the story about Nellie Grace's new baby shoes. But she'd been dusting the shelves in the den one morning and took down the shoebox with one new white shoe inside while he was sitting there. She told him about the shoe.

She had bought the little baby girl the new white Sunday shoes. She had quarreled with her husband, the baby's daddy, and to keep her home that Sunday, he'd angrily tossed one of the new baby shoes on top of the house. Neither she nor her husband ever made an attempt to take the shoe down. So the little shoe stayed there, partially hidden, a bitter reminder of a Sunday turned sour. If someone stood in a certain spot and turned their head just so, they could see it. But it took some doing even for Mae Lee, and she knew exactly where it was.

After she spilled out that particular story to Fletcher Owens, Mae Lee decided not to reveal any more family secrets. Her mama had always reminded her that a woman should hold back on a few things. Never tell a man everything about yourself. For a woman to always have a certain air of mystery, she had to hold back a little.

Then there was the singing. He loved to sing and had a

good singing voice and so did she. They seemed to sing almost the way they started to speak, with one voice. There were so many little things she liked about him, especially that he cupped his ear to listen to her. It made her feel he thought what she had to say was important.

But there were also some things about him that started to grate on her. The way he clicked his teeth when he was reading. Maybe she ought to buy him some Dentu Grip, she thought. The way he could sit for hours on end and twiddle his thumbs was annoying. She once asked if he ever tired of just sitting, twirling his thumbs over and over the same way. "Oh, yes," he'd said, and smiled. "But then I stop and twirl them the other way."

Later, she started to ask him something, but he was sound asleep, with his hands clasped across his chest. His full head of white hair was combed straight back, his strong face fully bared. His lower lip sagged slightly, but his mouth was closed, the furrows in his laugh line long and deep. His face was old only when he was asleep.

Whenever he talked about his coon dog, Colonel Yadkin, his face turned boyish. "Sure miss old Colonel Yadkin," he'd say. "That coon dog could tree a possum better than a possum hound."

One evening Mae Lee and Ellabelle sat in the semidark watching a quarter moon edge its way above the towering pines. Ellabelle slapped a mosquito biting away on her leg. "She's full of somebody's blood," she complained, wiping her fingers on an empty paper bag. "I hope she didn't fly up here from the house down near the railroad tracks. I don't want to catch nothing."

"She's been sucking up my blood all evening. All you'll probably catch is what I have, old age."

"I'm kind of hungry for something sweet," Ellabelle said, after a while. "Didn't you bake an egg custard yesterday?"

"I did," Mae Lee groaned, "but you seem to forget I have a boarder now."

"Oh," Ellabelle faked surprise, "is *that* what they are called nowadays?"

Mae Lee stiffened. "That wasn't nice, Ellabelle." She leaned forward in her rocking chair, lowering her voice to a concerned whisper. "People haven't started to talk, have they? They don't think that I'm . . . well, you know . . . ?"

"Oh, Lord no, Mae Lee, I'm just teasing," Ellabelle assured her.

Mae Lee leaned back, relieved. She took a deep breath and made her usual vain attempt to pull in her stomach. After all those years, it was nice to have a male presence in the house. It gave her a reason to dress up more often.

Fletcher Owens's arrival in Rising Ridge, South Carolina, had indeed brought about change in Mae Lee's life and thinking. She had almost forgotten that there were things to talk about other than children and cooking. She also realized how truly lonely she'd been before he came. His very presence was comforting.

She felt a sense of security with Fletcher Owens that she hadn't had with her husband. She imagined it would be really wonderful to be married to someone like Mr. Fletcher. The thought of marriage played on her mind, and she couldn't help wondering what her children might think. Especially her girls. She had the feeling that Taylor might be pleased.

Then, at half past seven in the evening, on the nineteenth of August, Fletcher Owens received a phone call. When he finished Mae Lee could tell he was nervous.

"I hate to get a call like this," he said. He frowned. "When a person gets older, it's hard on them to be put under this kind of pressure, to have someone just call and say come." He left the room.

Mae Lee heard Ellabelle's shuffling footsteps on the front porch. "Pick up your feet," she called out. "It's too early in the week for the lazy woman's shuffle."

Ellabelle slid into a chair. "I've been cleaning up my house. Getting ready to try and find me a mister to take in," she laughed.

Mae Lee didn't smile. "I believe my roomer is fixing to leave."

Mr. Fletcher appeared in the doorway. He wore the same gray pinstriped suit he'd worn the day he arrived, his coat draped across his arm. The top button of his clean white shirt was unbuttoned, the knot on his necktie loosened just below, shoes clean, but not shined.

Mae Lee liked that kind of look on a man. Obviously, Ellabelle did, too. "Lord have mercy, that's a pretty tie," she gushed, glancing at his worn suitcase. "Seems like you are fixing to travel, Mr. Fletcher?"

He looked worried. "I'm afraid I am," he said. "I'm going to have to catch that midnight train out of North Point tonight."

Mae Lee thought, that's a reserved train. "If you don't have a reservation you might not be able to get on that midnight train, Mr. Fletcher," she said.

"Oh, at this time of night, they'll find room for me," he said. He turned to face Mae Lee. "I've been called away. I don't think I'll be gone for more than a week or two." He forced a weak smile. "But I hope I can count on having a room when I get back. I'll leave my trunk with you, if it's all right."

Mae Lee felt a wave of relief sweep over her. "Oh, yes, Mr. Fletcher," she said, "you can count on your room being right here when you return."

"I'll need to get to North Point in order to catch that train. Is there a taxi I can call, Mae Lee?" he asked.

"Oh, I'll drive you," Ellabelle hurriedly spoke up.

Mae Lee glared at her friend. "I see my mouthpiece will be able to take you. I think I'll go along too."

Mae Lee rode in the front seat with Ellabelle. She tried to make light talk. "There's not too much traffic out this time of night, so we'll get you there in plenty time for the train, Mr. Fletcher."

"Good," he said quietly.

"I sure hate to see you pull up and leave on such notice, Mr. Fletcher," Ellabelle said sadly. "I hope you didn't forget anything."

Fletcher Owens was thoughtful for a few minutes, then he said, "Um-mmm, I think I left my old corncob pipe behind. Probably just as well I left it. I'm trying to quit. Smoked my pipe yesterday for the first time in a couple months," he said.

"It was nice knowing you, Mr. Fletcher Owens," Ellabelle said when they saw the train coming.

"Wait a minute," he smiled. "Like I said, I'll be back."

After the train pulled away, churning its streamlined cars through the darkness, Ellabelle still waved.

Mae Lee was impatient. "Are you going to stand there all night? It's well past midnight." Mae Lee watched Ellabelle shuffle to straighten her body, and although the train had long since disappeared into the darkness, Ellabelle pulled her fat legs into a proud strut.

"It's probably best that Fletcher Owens is going away for a while," Mae Lee said. "When he is around, you almost strut yourself to death."

On the way home Ellabelle asked Mae Lee where Mr. Fletcher was going. She couldn't believe that Mae Lee didn't know, and beyond that, hadn't even asked him. She also couldn't imagine how Fletcher Owens would leave without telling Mae Lee where he was going. "Most people don't leave the house where they live and not tell where they're going," she told Mae Lee.

She had fully intended to ask Mr. Fletcher where he was rushing out to in the middle of the night, but had kind of held back, waiting for him to say. And it seemed the next thing she knew, he was on that train and gone.

But he had asked her to save his room. She also remembered he'd left his trunk behind. "He'll be back," she told Ellabelle.

* * *

It was one-thirty in the morning when they drove up to Mae Lee's house. "See you in the morning," Ellabelle said, then laughed. "It *is* the morning."

Knowing that her boarder wasn't there seemed to make the house even emptier than before. She was alone in her house, her children long gone, now Mr. Fletcher as well. Maybe I should get a dog, or a cat, or a parrot or something, she thought, just so there will be something living in the house with me. She went to bed, but lay awake for a long time, hearing the night noises outside, an occasional automobile on the highway down the way, the bell on the Presbyterian church steeple downtown ringing three o'clock, a dog barking off in the distance somewhere. But inside her own house, not a sound. She was all by herself in the dark.

Before sunrise Mae Lee got out of bed and cooked breakfast, but she only picked at the grits, bacon, and eggs on her plate. She looked at the empty chair facing her. Mr. Fletcher had roomed in her house for only nineteen days, but she missed him. She would be glad when he returned.

It seemed having Mr. Fletcher out of the house cleared her mind, unclogged her thinking. She hadn't been able to think straight for almost a month. Perhaps now she'd get back to her volunteer work at the hospital. Well, anyway, she was not without resources. She had money in the bank, and over five thousand dollars here in the home.

Maybe she should buy an automobile. Taylor could teach her how to drive it. If she had a car and could drive, she could have taken Mr. Fletcher to catch the train last night without needing Ellabelle to go along.

She thought of what Ellabelle had said about it being odd that Mr. Fletcher hadn't told her where he was going, or why. Ellabelle was trying to make her suspicious of Mr. Fletcher; perhaps Ellabelle was a little bit jealous. She wondered where Mr. Fletcher *was* going. Why did he have to leave so suddenly, without any warning? From what she had heard of his telephone conversation, money was involved. She could have loaned him a little money, but he hadn't asked her to do it. Of course Mr. Fletcher had no way of knowing how much money she kept hidden away right there in the house.

He *was* coming back. After all, he had left his trunk up in his room, hadn't he?

She rose to her feet. Slowly, she began to feel knots tightening in her stomach. This is silly, she told herself. She'd been watching too many shows on that TV set. She walked over to the earthenware vase by the front door, where she kept her umbrellas, and reached down into it for the cotton drawstring bag with the money.

It was not there. No, she remembered, she had moved it from the vase last Sunday and put it somewhere else. Behind the flour bin in the kitchen? She hurried into the kitchen, pulled the bin away from the shelf. It wasn't there.

She began to feel hot all over. Where had she last hidden the money? She swept a stack of magazines off the top of the old wooden chest in the hallway, opened it, pushed aside the toys she kept there for her grandchildren. The bag wasn't there, either.

Oh, Lord, she thought, oh, Lord. Where did I hide the money? I've forgotten where I put it the last time I hid it.

Something else that Ellabelle had said now flashed into her mind. Ellabelle had said that it seemed strange that Mr. Fletcher could be so sure of getting a seat on a reserved-seat train like the Southerner, when he had no reservation. It was true; he had seemed to go right aboard the train without so much as even asking the conductor whether there was any room for him inside. It was as if he already had a ticket, Ellabelle had said. But if—

She began tearing about the house, racing to the usual places where she had hidden the money in the past. Her throat was dry, her face was on fire. She could feel her heart inside her chest beating like an express train. Where had she last hidden the cotton bag with her five thousand dollars inside it? *Had Fletcher Owens gone off with her money?*

: 19 :

About eleven-thirty in the morning Ellabelle drove to Mae Lee's house. When she walked up the front porch steps, she noticed that the front door was ajar and the lights were on. She called out to Mae Lee and cautiously pushed the door open. The house was in shambles. Ellabelle screamed, "Oh, Lord, oh Lord. She's been robbed." She slammed the door closed and started backing her way toward the front steps. As she hurried toward her car, she caught sight of Mae Lee at the edge of a flower bed, down on her knees, pulling things from her garden basket.

Ellabelle hurried to Mae Lee's side. She dropped to her knees and put her arms around her friend, but Mae Lee sprang free, stood up, and backed away like a frightened animal.

Ellabelle grabbed a firm hold on her.

"Poor baby," she moaned. "What's wrong?" She looked at Mae Lee's torn dress. "Who did this to you? When did it happen?"

Mae Lee only stared at her.

218

Ellabelle started screaming. "Oh, my Lord, you've been attacked, I'm calling the police! Oh, no, I'm taking you to the hospital. You look like you're having a stroke." Beads of sweat poured from Mae Lee's body; she gasped for her breath. Ellabelle grabbed Mae Lee's arm. "You're coming with me."

Mae Lee was like a child. She settled into the front seat of the car. Ellabelle fastened a seat belt around her shaking body.

"I don't know where it is," Mae Lee whispered. "I don't know where it is."

"Where what is?"

Mae Lee didn't reply for a minute. "It's gone," she finally said.

"Oh, Lord, Mae Lee you are starting to talk out of your head," Ellabelle moaned.

Fortunately, Dr. Bell was already at the hospital, on call for another patient. He checked Mae Lee's blood pressure and shook his head. "It's way up. I'm going to have to keep you here for a while," he said. "We will need to run some tests." Mae Lee was breathing normally again.

"Oh no, oh no," she repeated over and over. "I've got to go home, doctor. I've got to go home."

She stood up and backed against a table, sending a tray crashing to the floor and a nurse rushing into the room.

The doctor took her hand. "Something is wrong. What's upsetting you so much?"

Mae Lee's eyes searched his face as if for some flicker of hope. "It's, it's . . ." she broke off and turned her face away.

"Something has happened to one your children. I'll try to reach one of them."

Mae Lee turned to face him. "No! Don't call my children!"

Tears streamed down her cheeks. "Promise you won't call them. I swear I won't eat any more pork meat again."

Dr. Bell frowned. "There is something that's upsetting you and it's not pork meat."

He took her blood pressure again. He took Mae Lee's hand. "Mae Lee, your blood pressure is too high. I can't let you go home without running some tests. I think it's best for you to stay here. Let the nurse give you a sedative so you can get some rest. We'll see how things are later on."

Ellabelle didn't wait to hear what Dr. Bell had to say about Mae Lee's condition. She called Taylor.

She started crying as soon as Taylor answered the phone. "Taylor, baby," she cried, "you've got to come home. It's your mama. She's bad off, she's talking out of her head."

"What happened to her? Where is she? Is she all right?" Taylor's voice cracked. "Ellabelle, please don't cry."

"I brought your mama to the hospital. Dr. Bell is with her now. I have to go now. Just come, Taylor."

Ellabelle rushed up to Dr. Bell when he entered the hall. "I called Mae Lee's son. He is on his way here. What's wrong with her, doctor?"

Dr. Bell shook his head. "I don't know. Do you have any idea what caused her to become so disturbed?"

Ellabelle started wringing her hands. "To save my life I can't figure out what happened to her. At first, I had the notion she'd been robbed. But then when I saw her condition, I didn't stop to check things out." Ellabelle glanced at several of Mae Lee's concerned coworkers, anxiously waiting to learn about Mae Lee's condition. She dropped her voice, "Dr. Bell, did you notice that her dress was torn? Some crazy maniac didn't, didn't . . ." her voice trailed off.

Dr. Bell read Ellabelle's concerns. "No. There were no signs of having been exposed to violence of any kind."

Mae Lee was asleep under sedation when Taylor reached the hospital. After the nurses and hospital volunteers assured him that Mae Lee would receive their very special attention, he left with Ellabelle.

At his mother's house, Taylor helped Ellabelle straighten things out, and tried to make some sense of what might have happened. Why had clothes been pulled from closets, groceries and pots and pans from pantry shelves, pieces of furniture been moved around, and the interior of the house generally taken apart? It was as if his mother had had a fit or something, and in her frenzy had pulled everything out. And, if his mother had not done it, then who had? Robbery seemed unlikely, if only because Mae Lee's purse lay on the coffee table in the living room, untouched, with forty dollars inside.

He called his sisters and told them that their mother was in the hospital, and that tests were going to be run, but that Dr. Bell did not believe that things were grave enough for them to come rushing down to Rising Ridge. But within six hours of his calls, all four sisters were there. They met with Dr. Bell and several other physicians on the hospital staff. Other than the fact that Mae Lee's blood pressure was up, Dr. Bell told them, there were no physical symptoms to indicate anything abnormal about their mother's condition. His first thought, he said, was that she had suffered a stroke, but thus far tests had shown none of the indicators that accompanied strokes. Once Mae Lee had awakened from the sedation she had seemed normal, except that she couldn't—or wouldn't—talk, other than to say emphatically that she wanted to go home. They were going to keep her in the hospital for another twenty-four hours in order to run some more tests, but if no further evidence of physiological damage or impairment was turned up, Mae Lee might as well be taken home. "It's as if your mother has experienced some kind of emotional trauma," Dr. Bell said, "and is in a state of shock."

Mae Lee's children were afraid that if all five of them trooped into the hospital room together, their mother would be frightened and would think that she was seriously ill. When she got home, she would find them all there, but not until after Taylor and Annie Ruth had explained that they had been worried when they were told she was in the hospital, and had insisted on coming to see her.

Mae Lee's passivity was baffling. Taylor, Annie Ruth, and Ellabelle took turns staying with her in the hospital. She lay in her bed taking little notice of what was going on. When they tried to talk with her, she scarcely answered. From a medical standpoint there seemed to be nothing wrong with her.

Outside, in the hallway, they kept trying to understand what could have happened. Ellabelle told about how they had taken Fletcher Owens to the train, but insisted that there had been nothing unusual about Mae Lee's behavior either then or on the drive back to Rising Ridge. Whatever had happened, it seemed, must have taken place after she had returned home. But what could it have been? The doctors at the hospital could find nothing. Yet here was their mother, who had always been so capable, so full of life and in control of everything, lying in her bed, seemingly uncomprehending, like a child.

On the scorching-hot day that Mae Lee was discharged from the hospital, Taylor, Annie Ruth, and Ellabelle helped her down the hallway, out through the lobby, and into the car. The ladies of the hospital auxiliary stood by to give assistance if needed. Mae Lee hardly noticed them. When they arrived home, her three other daughters were waiting for her. Fletcher Owens's trunk had been moved out into the hallway and a rollaway bed placed in the room he had used, so that Dallace and Nellie Grace could stay there. Amberlee and Annie Ruth would sleep in the double bed in another room, and Taylor set up a cot on the sun porch for himself.

After Mae Lee had been taken to her room and was being installed in her bed, Taylor stood out in the hallway staring at Fletcher Owens's trunk, then shrugged his shoulders and joined Amberlee and Nellie Grace on the front porch. He didn't share his thoughts. After a while Ellabelle and Dallace came out and joined them. "Your mother's asleep now," Ella-belle said softly. "I can't bear to watch her lie there like a little helpless baby. But at least she seems less agitated, now that she's home."

"I'm not sure we should have brought her home," Dallace said. "I think she's had a stroke, no matter what they say. I really think we should have moved her to a hospital in Charlotte."

"We can still take her," Nellie Grace put in quickly. Annie

Ruth, however, shook her head. "Mama won't go. You would think that with all the new medical research, the doctors could say what's wrong with Mama—whether she's had a stroke or not. It seems to me her confused state of mind proves that's what probably happened. We've all heard what effect there is on older people when the brain is deprived of oxygen for just a short time."

Ellabelle didn't agree. "I believe if Mae Lee had had a stroke the doctors down at the hospital would have known it. Clairene's mama was rushed there a few weeks ago, and they said right off she'd had a stroke. They didn't have a speck of trouble pinpointing the problem," she said.

Nellie Grace shook her head sadly. "Maybe Clairene's mama didn't have old Dr. Bell. He's been practicing for so long, sometimes I question whether he's really competent. Older people aren't very open-minded and can't always keep up with what's new."

Ellabelle looked over the top of the sunshades resting on her nose. "Dr. Bell didn't decide it by himself. He called in young Dr. Gregory, who is well known and highly respected around here." She shifted uneasily in her chair. She could see that Mae Lee's children weren't impressed by him, either.

Taylor walked inside to look in on his mama, and promptly returned. "She's still asleep," he said. He pulled a chair forward and sat backward to face them, holding on to the back rail as though he needed it for support. "She seems restless even when she's sleeping," he said. "I think we ought to try and get her over to Charlotte as soon as we can."

Ellabelle shook her head. "Annie Ruth is right. Mae Lee won't go. Give her a little time to come to herself, children. See what happens." They agreed that Ellabelle was right. It would be very hard to get her to agree to go; still, something had to be done.

The house was within the city limits, yet from the corner of the porch where Taylor was sitting, the view opened out to uncultivated farmland. Parched, open fields that spread out empty and unproductive, like their own thoughts. Taylor gazed at a flower bed, filled with blooming flowers in spite of the grass that almost choked them out. Earlier, after the peonies had bloomed, his mama had asked him to weed. He'd never gotten around to it. Taylor thought about Fletcher Owens's trunk still in the house, and how well and happy his mama had been the last time he had visited. He also thought about his own failure to find out more about the roomer.

"Ellabelle," Taylor asked, "how much do you know about Fletcher Owens?"

Ellabelle shrugged her shoulders. "Probably no more than you or your mama. He was a nice respectable man, it seemed. Still, there's one thing about him that still eats on my nerves the way sour apples set my teeth on edge. It was the way he just up and left." She had the girls' attention now too. "He didn't say a word to Mae Lee that he was going to leave until the night he got the call to leave for the station. Then he didn't say where he was going, or when he was coming back."

Taylor stood up. "Ellabelle, I'm going to visit Cousin Warren and a few people. If you don't mind cooking something, I do believe I'll be hungry when I get back." Dallace volunteered to go along, while the others stayed behind to help Ellabelle with the cooking.

"I'm afraid you won't find out much from Warren," Ellabelle told them. "Mae Lee said he's getting awfully vague."

When Taylor and Dallace got to Warren's house, they were disappointed to find him so confused. Warren had been in poor health when they'd visited earlier in the summer, but he hadn't been disoriented. Now, however, when they asked him about Fletcher Owens, he looked at his wife, Lou Esther, and asked, "Do we know this man Owens?" Then without waiting for her to answer, he turned the conversation back to the old days. "You've got a smart mama, she's got a good business head on her shoulders. One of the best. She knows how to make a dollar and how to save it. Of course, I helped her out with handling the money. I insisted that she put her money in the bank. Thank the Lord she listened. I drove her over to the bank myself; she put every penny in. Mae Lee always did listen to me."

Warren turned to face Taylor. "She put the boy's name on the bank account with hers. You see, he lived the closest to her," he said, as if he were talking to someone other than Taylor. He raised his eyes to look beyond the young man. "I miss seeing my little buddy, but he'll come back to see me one day."

Warren was confused, but he was right about one thing—Mae Lee had indeed put Taylor's name on the bank account all those long years ago. Taylor had forgotten all about it, but Dallace remembered. She cast a questioning look at her brother. She wondered if he was thinking what she was. Fletcher

Owens might have been a con man. Had he gone off with their mother's life savings?

Taylor looked at his watch. "We hate to rush away, Cousin Warren, but we have to get back home," he said.

Taylor was locked on target now. Dallace almost had to run to keep up with Taylor as he hurried to the car. "We've got to get to the bank."

At the bank the manager, Jackson Rowe, was ready to lock the door when Dallace and Taylor rushed up, but he let them inside. Taylor checked the joint account. There had been no withdrawals for some months, since well before Fletcher Owens came to town. So, they were back where they started.

"I still think Fletcher Owens might be involved in this," Taylor declared. "I wonder where he's gone?"

"Ellabelle said he didn't tell them," Dallace said.

"I wish we knew more about him," Taylor said.

After supper Mae Lee's children made the decision that Annie Ruth was right; her mama should stay with her in Greensboro, but first she should be taken to the Duke University Hospital for testing. Annie Ruth's sister-in-law, a registered nurse at Duke Hospital, would be asked to arrange to get her admitted for a checkup there. The only trouble now was, who would tell their mama about the plans?

All day and the next the children stayed close to their mother, taking turns at Mae Lee's bedside. Mae Lee had nothing to say to them. They worried about her. She had always been overjoyed when they were home again; now it seemed to make no difference to her. Obviously something was very wrong. What was going through her mind, they wondered. She seemed to be off somewhere in a world of her own. Or was *anything* going through her mind? Did she even know that they *were* there, all of them? Did she understand that? Did she realize that there was anything unusual about their all being there at home with her? They couldn't tell. All they could do was to stay with her, looking after her wants, making sure that somebody was at the bedside at all times.

: 20 :

What her children could not know, of course, was that not only was Mae Lee perfectly aware of their presence in the house, but the one thing she wanted was for them *not* to be there—to leave her alone, so that she could continue to look for the money. She was sure it was somewhere in the house, but where? Where had she hidden it? She couldn't believe that Mr. Fletcher had taken her $5,240.22. But where had Mr. Fletcher gone off to, so suddenly and with no explanation? If Mr. Fletcher *had* taken her money—the very thought made her groan inwardly. Had she made a fool of herself, fallen for the man, been taken in by him, when all that he had been after was her money?

After all these years, had she once again allowed herself to be fooled by a man?

She needed to tell someone that the money was gone. Later, alone with Ellabelle, she had almost summoned up enough courage to do it. "Ellabelle," she began timidly, "have you ever done anything so dumb and stupid that you couldn't bring yourself to tell anyone about it?"

The very question seemed to open up the floodgates for Ellabelle. She poured out so many stories she had wanted to tell someone that by the time she finished, Mae Lee had lost her nerve.

She needed to find her money, and the only way she would be able to look for the missing money was to get everybody out of the house somehow.

She lay in silence, listening. Suddenly she had an idea; it might be that she had left the bag with the money in it up on the very top shelf of the pantry. That was one place she had not looked. She listened, and thought about it. The children were apparently all outside on the front porch. If only Ellabelle would go out and join them.

She closed her eyes, pretended to be asleep, occasionally opening one eyelid just a crack to see if Ellabelle were seated there by the bed. After a while she heard a noise, and peeked out to see Ellabelle tiptoeing out of the room. She heard her walk down the hall, and then the sound of the front porch door opening and shutting. Quickly she got up, hurried into the kitchen, set a chair next to the pantry shelf, and climbed up on it. She pushed aside jars of preserved peaches and plums lining the shelf, groped with her hand along the back wall. The bag was not there.

"Mama!" It was Dallace's voice. "What are you doing on that chair? Taylor!" she shrieked. "Come here!"

Taylor and Nellie Grace came hurrying into the room. Taylor stepped over to Mae Lee and helped her down to the floor. "Mama, what's going on?" he asked.

Mae Lee offered no explanation, and let herself be guided back into her room. As they helped her into bed, she tried to think of some way to tell her children about the money. Holding so much inside was painful for her. She started to speak, but the anxious lump in her chest tightened. She had difficulty breathing. She stared speechlessly at her children. She pulled her thoughts in even tighter. She felt as if she was having a terrible nightmare. She seemed unable to pinpoint a place for herself—a presence. It was almost as if her children were there, but she was somewhere else. She felt the tension and anxiety pound at her heart. In a futile attempt to fight back, she tightened the corners of her mouth, pulled her face into a mosaic of frowns, and closed her eyes.

She listened to Dallace phone Dr. Bell. She knew he would come even if it wasn't convenient for him. Tears streamed down her cheeks. She looked at her daughters. Not only did they believe she was very ill, they thought she'd lost her mind. But then, how could they think otherwise? It tore so at her heart. How could she tell them that it wasn't her mind that was lost, but *five thousand two hundred and forty dollars and twenty-two cents*?

: 21 :

It was Sunday afternoon. Mae Lee and her children had already eaten. Ellabelle had cooked, as was her custom, parts of Saturday and early Sunday morning. Anxious to get her work behind her, she'd urged the family to eat as soon as she finished baking her hot rolls. "It's double work for a cook to have to wait, then turn around and heat up," she complained.

Mae Lee didn't get back into bed after dinner. She sat in the living room with her children and Ellabelle. For a while, the group kept up the chatter they'd started at dinner. Mae Lee looked on, knowing that her children were not cheerful and that they also knew it. *She* certainly wasn't cheerful, and she made no effort to pretend. She had abandoned all plans to tell about the missing money. She knew that she would never get up enough courage to do that, much less tell about her fear that Fletcher Owens had gone off with it. She would take the secret with her to her grave, she decided. She had been tricked, fooled by a con man, who had obviously seen her hiding the money, waited for the right moment, then arranged for someone to telephone him, so that he could make a hurried departure. There's no fool like an old fool, all right, she thought.

She was also worried because she couldn't remember where it was that she had last placed the money, so that Fletcher Owens had seen her hiding it there. Perhaps she *was* losing her mind, or at least her memory. She worked to convince herself that she could still remember something. She went over the names of the volunteers down at the hospital, and even the names of the relatives of her deceased former husband, Jeff Barnes, counting them off on her fingers as she named them silently to herself.

A hushed quiet settled in. Mae Lee's children wished they hadn't told everyone who called, and had the pastor to announce at services, that Mae Lee had been ordered by the doctors to rest and not have visitors. A house full of company might have been nice on a quiet Sunday afternoon. At least it would have been more cheerful, perhaps. Maybe Mae Lee's friends from the hospital would have visited and cheered her up.

Lost in thought, Mae Lee's children looked to each other for answers to unspoken questions. How would they approach their mama about going to the hospital in Durham, North Carolina? Annie Ruth worried that her husband might complain that he would end up getting stuck with the bills if her mama ended up with them for a while. She refused to let her thinking go beyond that, however. She watched her older sister's face. There was a slight twitch; Dallace was nervous. Annie Ruth wondered what she was thinking about.

Dallace was thinking about the hospital in Durham, too, but she entertained little hope that her mother would benefit from a stay there. After she and Taylor visited Warren, she'd concluded that, like him, her mama was probably in the early stages of Alzheimer's disease.

Amberlee sidled up to her mama and pressed her cheek against her hair. "I took down that old man's portrait in my apartment, Mama," she said. "I don't need a grandfather half as much as I need you, Mama."

Mae Lee nodded, but her face didn't register happiness. She was watching Nellie Grace pretend to read a magazine. She hadn't turned a page since she opened it.

Nellie Grace's thoughts were fastened on the note they'd found that Mae Lee had written to them, begging them not to put her into a nursing home. Perhaps her mama knew that she was saddled with something incurable. Maybe Dr. Bell knew too. They had all read and reread the note, and had mentally penciled in their own thoughts and meanings. Nellie Grace thought of her mama climbing up on the chair in the pantry for no reason whatever. Mama's really sick, she thought, and it's not all in her mind.

Everyone was trying not only to be cheerful, but also to say the right thing. Ellabelle, however, failed to notice that. Out of the still afternoon quiet, she abruptly announced that she'd heard in broad daylight the voice of the rarely heard evening whippoorwill. She pressed a finger against her lips and signaled quietness for the already quiet group. She was clearly disturbed. "I don't like this one single bit," she said, peering through the window at the sunlit sky. "That whippoorwill usually calls just as darkness is descending and shortly before dawn. Often, if the moon is out, you can hear its voice during the night but almost never in daylight. It's a bad omen," she said, and without thinking, turned to Mae Lee. "It's a death warning when you hear the voice of a whippoorwill in broad daylight. Did you hear it, Mae Lee?" Mae Lee shook her head.

"You had to hear it," Ellabelle insisted. "I know I'm not hearing things. The loud sound is unmistakable. It rings out the three sounds of its name over and over so fast it doesn't catch its breath." Her eyes searched faces. No one else had heard the whippoorwill, but what Ellabelle had said cast a pall over the room.

Ellabelle grew quiet. She clenched her fists and dropped her head. She sat thinking about what she'd said. How could she have even spoken about death to Mae Lee?

The stillness disturbed Taylor. It was only five o'clock; the afternoon had seemed to stretch out for hours. He stole furtive looks at his mama. The blank stare on her face was puzzling, almost frightening. It was as if she were a stranger. She seemed to have aged so quickly. Maybe she'd looked that way for some time and he hadn't paid any attention. He could only mull over "if only"—if only they had done this, or that. He needed to call his wife to tell her that he and his sisters would be staying on for another night until they could get Mae Lee to agree to go to a bigger hospital.

The television had been turned on but no one really watched. Their efforts to appear cheerful were failing miserably. They tried to talk normally, yet they spoke in whispers, and almost tiptoed when they moved about. Conversations started but quickly ended.

A light knock at the front door went unnoticed, as though it were just another TV sound. The second time, the clang of the heavy virgin brass knocker on the front door was louder and clearer. Taylor opened the front door.

A tall, thin, gray-haired man stood outside the door, a suitcase in one hand and another one on the porch floor beside him.

: 22 :

"**M**r. Owens!" It was Taylor who spoke first.

Fletcher Owens was clearly taken aback by the circle of people seated in the room. He recognized Ellabelle, and nodded to her and then to Mae Lee. There was a moment of embarrassed silence, then Taylor picked up the other suitcase from the porch and brought it inside.

"I'm afraid you weren't expecting me, Mrs. Barnes," Fletcher Owens said to Mae Lee. "I wasn't coming until later in the week, but I was able to get a ride from High Point, so I decided to come on today."

Mae Lee stared at him. Taylor hurriedly introduced the other members of the family. There was a long pause. Then Mae Lee half rose from her chair.

"Mr. Fletcher, where's my money?" she demanded.

"Your money?" Fletcher Owens seemed puzzled. "I don't owe you any rent money, do I?"

"I'm talking about my five thousand two hundred and forty dollars and twenty-two cents!"

237

"Mama, what are you talking about?" several of the daughters chorused.

"This is between Mr. Fletcher and me," Mae Lee said firmly.

"I don't understand what you mean," Fletcher Owens told her. "Do you mean you've lost some money?"

Nobody spoke.

"Mama, what's going on?" Taylor finally said. "Is there some money missing?" He looked at her, then at Fletcher Owens, who appeared to be baffled.

Fletcher Owens frowned. "I think I understand now." He looked across the room. "The last time I saw you move it, I believe you put it here. Not that it means anything. It seems like you moved it every day." He walked over to the earthenware umbrella stand, paused, and lifted out several umbrellas. "No," he said, speaking half to himself. He thought for a moment, then walked over to where Amberlee was sitting. "Would you mind getting up for a minute, Miss?" he asked.

Amberlee stood up and moved out of the way. He reached down into the torn upholstery of Mae Lee's old overstuffed chair. "Here it is," he said. He pulled out a cotton drawstring bag, and handed it to Mae Lee. "Is this what you have in mind?"

"What's all this about, Mr. Owens?" Taylor asked. "What's in the bag?"

"Your mother," Fletcher Owens told him, "evidently thought that I went off with the money she keeps in that bag. Is that right, Mrs. Barnes?"

Mae Lee's expression was an odd mixture of joy and pain. Then tears welled and overflowed her eyes.

"We thought she had a stroke," Taylor explained to Fletcher Owens. "The day after you left, something happened to her. They couldn't find anything wrong with her at the hospital, but it's been like she'd lost her mind or something. She wouldn't tell us what was wrong. And all the time, it was this money which she must have been keeping hidden here in the house, and we didn't even know existed. She must have forgotten where she kept it, and she thought . . ."

"That I'd stolen it," Fletcher Owens finished the explanation for him.

Now Ellabelle pulled herself up to all of her full, righteous glory. "What was she supposed to think?" she demanded. "You just up and left without hardly saying scat. Didn't say where you were going, or why. Like a thief in the night. Then her money turns up missing, or she thinks it's missing. Isn't that right, Mae Lee?"

Mae Lee only covered her eyes with her hands and sobbed. Taylor knelt down next to her chair and put his arm around his mother. "It's all right, Mama," he said. "We understand."

"Well," Ellabelle puffed, "if this isn't the damnedest thing I've ever seen. Here we are sitting around getting ready for a funeral, and talking about sending Mae Lee to the hospital up in Durham, and all the time Mae Lee and Mr. Fletcher have only had some crazy misunderstanding. Simply because neither one of them had the brains to tell anybody else what was going on!"

Fletcher Owens shook his head sadly. "It wasn't very thoughtful of me," he said. "I did leave my trunk behind, but I should have explained where I was going. My daughter in

239

High Point was about to have a baby, and her husband was out of the country and there was nobody else to take care of her children." He turned to Mae Lee. "I'm truly sorry for the mix-up, but I'm getting to be an old man, and I tend to forget that others can't read my mind."

"We are all getting old, I'm afraid," Ellabelle said.

Now everybody began talking at once. "Won't you sit down, Mr. Owens?" Dallace asked. "I'm sorry we're in such confusion."

"Thank you," Fletcher Owens said, "but I've been traveling most of the day, and I'm very tired. If it's all right, I'll just go on to my room."

"Your room?" Dallace was obviously embarrassed. "I'm afraid that we weren't expecting you, and . . ."

"Mr. Owens," Taylor quickly broke in, "the girls have been staying in your room, but if you don't mind, you could sleep on the sun porch tonight, and they'll be out of there tomorrow morning."

"No, I can stay at a motel tonight," Fletcher Owens said. "I don't want to cause any more disruption than what I've already caused. If you'll just let me use the phone, I'll call a taxicab."

"It's no disruption," Taylor assured him. "I've been sleeping out there, but I'm going straight back to my family, now that Mama's all right again." He picked up the two suitcases. "There's plenty of room for you. You just come right along with me."

After Fletcher Owens had excused himself and gone out to the sun porch, and Taylor had told his mother and sisters good-bye and departed for home, Mae Lee and her daughters and Ellabelle sat in the living room and talked. Mae Lee had stopped crying, and after a while she began to seem like her old self again, although obviously she was still feeling embarrassed about what had happened.

"If it hadn't caused so much grief and pain," Ellabelle declared, "this whole thing would be funny. Shame on you," she said to Mae Lee, "getting yourself all worked up over a man at your age!" She laughed.

"Was it the man, or the money?" Annie Ruth asked.

"I'd say it was a little of both," Amberlee said.

"What I don't understand, Mama," Dallace said, "is why you were keeping the money in the house in the first place, instead of putting it in the bank like Warren said he told you to do?"

"I should have listened to him," Mae Lee agreed. She held up the bag with the money in it. "Tomorrow this is going in the bank, every cent of it. Even the twenty-two cents." She rose to her feet. "It's past my time for me to be going to bed, too. It's been a long day for all."

: 23 :

The sound of a buzzing chain saw drifted across the countryside. It was the sound of fall. Soon winter's cold would swallow up the fall afternoons and pull them into early darkness.

Mae Lee and Ellabelle sat on the front porch. It was time for their yearly watch for the migrating Canada geese flying south. They looked forward to those rare glimpses of the beautiful creatures, the sudden chorus of honking overhead. For years it had been a time they shared. They never made a conscious effort to make it a special occasion. There was no need to; the occasion created itself. They pulled warm wraps tightly about their bodies.

"A cup of hot cider or cocoa would be nice right now," Mae Lee said.

"A piece of sweet potato custard pie would even be better," Ellabelle put in. "But with Mr. Fletcher rooming here, I bet there's not a sliver left in the house."

The women watched the fall sky. The telephone rang.

"The phone's ringing, Mae Lee," said Ellabelle.

"It's okay," Mae Lee said, "they'll call back." Even so, Ellabelle got up to answer the ringing phone.

Mae Lee's thoughts were beyond who might be calling. Mr. Fletcher had told her he had finally gotten a clear title to the land he'd inherited off Butterchurn Road just beyond Catfish Creek, the land that his daddy's brother had left him. He'd held on to it for years. "It's way off the main course," he'd said, "just a stretch of land on the way to somewhere, but it's a nice little piece of ground, good farmland. Might plant me a little vegetable garden in the spring."

Mae Lee also owned land alongside Catfish Creek. Visions of the creek teeming with catfish, and fields of fresh tomatoes, peas, and silver queen corn danced in her head.